PERMISSION GRANTED

Kenneth W Frankland, scholar, artist, and teacher was born in Huddersfield in 1944.

ISBN-13: 978-1517481780

ISBN-10: 1517481783

Copyright © Neal Stuart Wilson Frankland 2015

2 Carleton Park Avenue, Pontefract, West Yorkshire, United Kingdom, WF8 3RH

Permission Granted

Kenneth W Frankland

To

Neal Stuart Wilson Frankland

And

Phyllis Mary Frankland

Part One

– – –

Chapter One

'What I like about England', said Irma, 'is that you can say exactly what you please to people and nobody is the teeniest bit offended. Why back home you have to think twice before you blow your nose.'

If this was really the case, Letitia wondered, how had the speaker managed to get in the enormous amount of practice which must have been necessary to achieve her present fluency?

Irma Quakke took an unaccustomed and, alas, only momentary breather, while she tugged neurotically at her new tartan mini-skirt, bought only a week ago, which left a gap between the top of her knees and an imaginary line a foot higher up her thighs which she described as the plimsoll line. She had thought she felt a rather strong draught in the aforementioned area but, recognising in it the cold breath of Puritanism, she prepared to speak again and began stroking her thighs for warmth with long-nailed fingers. A quick glance to see that there was no danger of snagging her tights in the operation and she launched into the peroration.

'I was only saying to Hymie yesterday what a fruitful field for his studies on permissivism in the modern society this old country of yours was. 'Hymie,' I said, I call him Hymie for short, 'Hymie,' I said, 'Here's something you can really get your balls into.' '

The voice droned on for several minutes and various obscenities more. Letitia Mann was trying not to listen. While this talkative young woman appeared to think she was using the everyday speech of permissive Britain in the sixties, it was, nevertheless, not the currency of Tolbridge Rectory.

Eventually Letitia's eyebrows tried to close the subject. 'Are you settling in alright now, Mrs Quakke? I hope you don't find our environment, well, too restraining.' She had tried to find a reproach, but it had not been in her.

'Oh, we're settling in just fine dear, and I just love the little old cottage we've rented. Of course, one does miss the deep-freeze – so handy having half a side of beef there when you want it, don't you think? And things are so much cheaper over here. I'm sure Hymie thinks it's all worth it in any case, although it was me who persuaded him to come over in the first place. The dear boy is so shy you just wouldn't believe it.

'Oh really,' replied Letitia, who was quite prepared to believe it and to hazard a guess at some of the reasons for it. How on earth could she find a way of closing the conversation without appearing too rude? She fell back on the unconvincing formula which her husband, in his capacity as professional reassurer, always seemed to use. 'Well, I do hope you enjoy the rest of your stay with us, Mrs Quakke.'

'I'm sure we shall, dear. I'm sure we shall.'

A glint of hope came into Letitia's eye as she sipped her second cup of tea. There had now been a silence of almost twenty seconds and it very much resembled the uneasiness which precedes a parting – then a voice on her left broke open the illusion.

'Do tell us more about your husband's work, Mrs Quakke. It must be fascinating to be married to such a clever man.' The speaker was Lucy Lastick, dark, very attractive, wife of Titus Lastick, chairman of Sapling Fibres and thirty years older, if not wiser, than herself. 'I wonder what he's like in bed,' she was musing about the shy Mr Quakke. 'I must make a note to find out.'

'I should like to meet him,' she continued aloud.

'Well, nice of you to say so, Mrs Lastick' – she pronounced it 'Lasteeke', a faulty emphasis perhaps expected from an American, but found none the less hard to tolerate – 'Being in contact with Hymie all the time I find it difficult to look upon him as clever (others, it was true, had the same difficulty) but he has his ideas, he has his ideas.'

Lucy, who had only one, situated in a rather comfortable position between her legs, was both intrigued and amazed. She leant forward in her chair to show her interest.

'For instance,' drawled Irma, 'he has this quaint little idea that all this permissiveness is ruining young people.'

'Oh, I do so agree,' put in Letitia Mann who was beginning to think she had misjudged the poor woman and was about to pour her another cup of tea and offer her a buttered scone by way of compensation. She grasped the tea-pot so non-permissively she nearly broke the china handle.

'Yeah, well, he says it's not permissivity at all. I mean they think they can do what they like, but it's really an ego foisted on them by the older generation who, as an outlet for their own condemnation complex, have forced them to behave in the way they do.'

'How interesting,' shuddered Letitia, replacing the silver cake tray on which the last buttered scone quivered as a protest against its mistress' indecision or perhaps out of relief at escaping those super-efficient American jaws. 'And what does your husband see as the solution to this problem?' went on the hostess, prolonging the conversation in spite of herself.

'Very simple. They've just got to work it out for themselves, dear. He'll help them to break away from this generation-gap tyrannicism, of course. So, as a matter of fact, that's why he's over here – to write a book exposing the whole situation. But their salvation, he tells me time and time again, will only come from themselves.'

'I see,' said Lucy, whose vision – truth to tell – had been rather blurred by the jargon of psycho-anthropoid sociology and whose ability to follow the conversation had ended at 'balls'.

'I suppose then,' Letitia crossed her legs defensively and broke the etiquette of a whole generation by putting the last scone out of its misery, 'each individual must find his own solution.'

Lucy imagined she was back in the conversation again.

'Oh no. Forgive me, Mrs Mann,' Irma smiled indulgently, 'but you clergypersons do see things in black and white whereas the field of psycho-anthropoid sociology is really rather a pretty shade of grey. Hymie says it is only by the self-abnegation and reassertion of the ego through the group complex that these kids can really do their own thing.'

Lucy sat dumb, but still interested. Mrs Mann was losing ground. Her fingers toyed noiselessly with a necklace of artificial pearls which nestled comfortably in her matronly bosom. Finally, in desperation... 'Er, would you like another cup of tea, Mrs Quakke. I do find these conversations stimulating, but thirsty work, don't you think?'

'Thank you very much, my dear. It's been simply lovely having an English tea in this lovely old English vicarage, but I really must be going now. Poor Hymie will be there all alone at home writing up his research and I expect the shy boy will just be longing for my approval of it.'

'What an extraordinary woman,' confided Letitia to Lucy when with a last tug at her mini-skirt Irma Quakke had disappeared through the front door and was frightening away the sparrows with the revs of her white Cadillac.

'Yes, extraordinary,' said Lucy. 'Her husband sounds rather sweet, though.'

'Christ!' swore Irma, as she sped down Tolbridge High Street, one hand on the wheel, the other straightening her hair in the driving mirror, 'this vicarage tea-party conversation sure bores the pants off you.'

– – –

Irma turned off the High Street into a road that was no more than a cart-track, lined on either side with clumpy nettles. Had not someone told her they encouraged bees and butterflies? Half-way along the track she parked the Cadillac in her own inimitable fashion, slammed the door hard and strode off eagerly up the crazy-paved path with its rose borders.

Scarcely four strides took her to the white front door. She gave an affectionate pat to the brass door knocker, an attractive piece of metal in the shape of a reclining Venus, whose ample breasts performed the outcome of their vernacular appellation.

Hymer Quakke had watched her from the window with that self-congratulatory pride men reserve for their own possessions. 'Impressive sight', he thought. 'Not many women of her age could look that good.' Her long, blond hair was as sleek and beautiful as ever. Her blue eyes sparkled as at their very first meeting. He continued the inventory: long, straight nose, broad, but not ugly, mouth, firm, small breasts, long slim legs. She might have been a Swede or a Dane. Yes she was really something as they said back home. He would have been ready to commit adultery with her, had he not already possessed her. What greater compliment could he possibly pay a woman of fortyish.

He saw her now, slightly breathless, pause at the door, give a snort with the impatience of the true extrovert and, not being able to find immediately the key which must be hiding somewhere in the debris of her handbag, search for a few minutes, then realizing the door was open anyway, push it further ajar and charge in like a randy stallion.

'Hymie dear, oh Hymie, cooee..!'

Quakke had at least had the sense of timing not to go and meet her at the door – he had once narrowly escaped being run over by a mad delegate to a Truckers' Convention – although it would have cost him little effort to reach the aperture, the dining-room in the small cottage being almost adjacent.

'Here, honeybunch,' he called, almost choking with the smoke from his favourite meerschaum pipe as he tried to shout with it in his teeth. He strolled over to the piano and began to strum Wagner's contribution to the marriage service which he always did when his wife approached, a quirk which did no lasting harm to anybody, irritated a good many and even amused some, especially since when a pianoforte was unavailable he would be likely to render his Wagnerian leitmotif on a harmonica drawn with the dexterity of a Randolph Scott from his breast pocket. Practice, of course, makes perfect and the operation usually went without a hitch, except on the odd occasion when, reaching into the putative holster he would find himself giving a silent, some said not unpleasant, performance on a spectacle case in B flat. When this happened he tended to regard it as a sad omen for his married life, which, however, had so far survived a few gauche tacets.

'Oh, sweetie you still love me!' cried the serenaded spouse, changing metaphors in mid-gallop, cascading through the minuscule lobby, flowing around Hymer and overwhelming him with hot, wet kisses to compensate for their unbearable separation of three hours.

'Well, honey, how did your tea party go?' gasped Quakke, breathing deeply but with some difficulty and giving his beloved a sharp slap on the left buttock. The perceptive reader will have realised that this was yet another of his little superstitions.

'Quite nice people, Hymie, a trifle stuffy, of course. Although they did seem quite receptive to your ideas. Anyway, I'm sure we'll all get along like a house on fire.'

'Great, that's just great!' He often repeated himself in case nobody had heard the first time for he spoke very quietly.

'Come and sit down on the couch and tell me what you've been doing all this time on your own.' Irma made up for her husband's lack of volume.

'Well, I guess I've spent the whole afternoon writing up the findings of our visit to Carnaby Street,' whispered Quakke. It really is most interesting, most interesting.

His wife eagerly nodded her encouragement.

'It seems to me... (hesitation as though perhaps he doubted his own supposition) It seems to me, although, of course, one cannot at this stage be categorical, that these teenagers have quite a marked tendency to be interested in dressing up.' He spoke as if he were writing a standard textbook. 'This is possibly anthropologically speaking a regressive recapitulation of some traumatic childhood experience.'

'Oh sure, Hymie, sure to be.' She was not sure at all whether he was using the right words, but decided not to comment. 'Please go on.'

'On the other hand, de-vestimentation-wise, there is a distinct proclivity to disrobe, displayed very prominently by the-er-brevity of the skirt.' His eyes strayed to the strikingly prominent display of Irma's legs, 'and the-er-revealing transparency of the upper garments, while in some cases-er- the mammary areas are completely –er –exposed to the elements...'

'Call it "tits", dear, everybody does over here,' put in Irma.

'... showing the-er-victory of the basic natural, maternal instinct at the expense of the socially acceptable preservation of what is termed "modesty".'

'And this will all go in your book, Hymer? I just can't wait to read it. I'm sure this time it will be a great success.'

'Yes, dear, I too am confident on this occasion,' said the psycho-sociological anthropologist, his mind going back to the piles of rejection slips littered like gravestones over the stacks of manuscripts in the closet back home. He remembered with painful clarity the ninety-five headstones for "The social rehabilitation of monks and nuns". He had been sure that was a winner too.

That adorable confidence-booster Mrs Quakke soon brought him back to earth again.

'After that you deserve your favourite English meal – egg and chips. I'll just go and slave over that hot stove for you, honey. Say... how about that for a song lyric?' And with an affectionate peck at the shiny dome of Quakke's head. 'Was it Abe Lincoln who said, "The way to a man's heart is through his stomach."?'

'No, dear, it was probably Nathalie Weinburger,' retorted Quakke with a concealed belch, half in anticipation of rivers of grease flowing over his plate, half in his contempt for his wife's lifelong friend and confidante who had a saying for every conceivable occasion of the Christian and Pagan year.

'Well, whoever it was,' laughed Irma gaily, 'I shall now prepare for your delight the most deelicious meal you ever ate in the whole of your life.'

'Probably the last,' mused Hymie.

Chapter Two

'One minute,' said the producer to Don Missmuch the television interviewer and Hymer Quakke the psycho-anthropological sociologist.

The latter was at that moment wondering how he had found himself exposed to one rather fierce looking interviewer, a whole studio crew, a sizeable studio audience and several million viewers, oh my God, several million viewers. His eyes behind thick spectacles felt sore from the lights and he was afraid that the sweat, beginning to burst from his pores, would ruin his make-up. The invitation had come about a fortnight ago. The picture was rather confused. Why had he accepted? – NO, HE HADN'T – NO, THAT'S RIGHT, HE HADN'T ACCEPTED. Irma had done it for him. He remembered now. It was the evening after she came back from the vicarage and she did her famous egg and chips. Yes, and he'd been in the bathroom when the call came and had just heard the beginning and end of a telephone conversation...

'Hello, Dr Quakke's secretary here...we...ll that's just fine... the 20th it is then at 9 o'clock... yes... Oh don't worry about that at all. Goodbye!'

He had been in the bathroom several more minutes and when he came downstairs, feeling more than a little fragile, and still rather bilious, he had just about had the curiosity to ask what the call was about, but certainly not the strength to resist any pressure.

Irma, however, had been full of it.

'Just fancy, sugar, they want you on television in a fortnight's time. I told you you were going to make a success of it this time, didn't I?'

'What? WHY?' Quakke managed to say.

'Well, it seems some old schlemil of a biologist/zoologist, whatever, Charles Beagle, Bugle...'

'Beagle, honey, one of the most eminent zoologists of our day. I'm surprised you never heard of him.'

'Any way, Beagle, Bugle has been taken ill quite suddenly, won't be about for months and they want someone to replace him at very short notice on "Tête à tête". (It was a sort of face to face programme in which world-shaking ideas were not elicited from the celebrity by the probing Missmuch). Someone kindly recommended you.'

'Yes, dear, very kind.'

It hadn't seemed very real then, something rather distant and it seemed even less real now if that were possible. The most tangible proof that something was going on, Hymer reflected, was a tall, blonde American lady sitting on the front row of the specially invited studio audience and waving at him with a passable imitation of a Churchill victory sign, at least it would have been passable, had the palm of her hand been facing outward instead of vice versa. For some reason the audience appeared to be tittering.

Now what was this character hunched over towards him saying? He felt as though he had come into the cinema half way through the movie.

'And so, ladies and gentlemen (you ignorant sods) while wishing Sir Charles a speedy recovery from the recurrence of his malaria (more like VD the randy old baronet) we welcome to "Tête à tête" (why can't we have a bloody English title?) someone I'm sure we are going to hear a lot more about. (We couldn't be that unlucky). He is an American and is over here to write a book on that ever present phenomenon which has puzzled us in this country (not me I'm enjoying it) for many years, that is the Permissive Society. Dr Hymer Quakke.'

A large sign saying 'Applause' was illuminated over the heads of the protagonists and the audience duly responded, none more warmly than the American on the front row.

Quakke managed to squeeze a feeble smile through lips that were pursed thoughtfully like the nozzle of a tube of toothpaste. He blinked at Irma behind his tortoiseshell spectacles with a look that could only signify tenderness or reproach.

'Dr Quakke,' this nuisance of a fellow opposite him was saying, with inappropriate emphasis, 'would you tell us first of all what exactly a psycho-anthropoid sociologist is?'

'Surely,' said Quakke, awakening to the sound of his description. 'A P.A.S., as we call them for short, studies the way man reacts mentally to his environment.' He vaguely remembered some textbook or other he happened to have read.

'I see and wouldn't you agree Dr Quakke (you will if you've any sense) that the pressures on modern man are greater than they have ever been before and that at almost every moment they appear to be increasing in intensity?'

'Surely,' replied Quakke. (Why doesn't he let me answer the questions?)

Don Missmuch, who looked upon the American's one word answer as a sign of his incompetence, was sharpening his long knives as he continued the interrogation. If the outright kill failed he could always try the slow torture.

'And wouldn't you agree also (God, what a bore!) that the task of the P.A.S. as you call him is in itself becoming more and more complex and more and more demanding as the pressures to er preserve certain standards of living, to maintain the status quo, to er meet the exigencies of a sexually orientated society, pile up on us?'

'Surely,' nodded Quakke for the third time, blowing a puff of smoke in Missmuch's direction which the latter did not expect any more than

Quakke intended it. It was perhaps the faithful meerschaum's own reaction to the conversation.

Quakke started to speak. 'I should have thought...'

'Doctor,' coughed Missmuch who was not going to have his next question spoiled by what anybody thought. He used the world "doctor" as he would have applied the term "minister" to a member of the cabinet, as if to imply the inadequacy of the title's bearer to fulfil the duties of the office. 'Doctor, time is running short I'm afraid (why do these chaps talk so much?) so can we move to the more specific reasons for your visit to this country. Tell us on the basis of your observations to date what conclusions you hope to come to.'

'Well,' drawled Quakke as he drew a deep breath and put his meerschaum in the ashtray. 'It seems to me. It seems to me, although of course one cannot at this stage be absolutely and irrevocably categoric, that there is in this permissive society of yours' ...the blonde in the front row was nodding vigorously... what might be anthropologically speaking a regressive recapitulation of the ordinary childhood experience. This, of course, manifests itself...'

'I'm sorry Doctor Quakke but I shall have to cut you off there. I'm sure viewers will have enjoyed hearing your fascinating views. Thank you for coming along and joining us on "Tête à tête". I trust that the rest of your stay with us will be both pleasant and fruitful and we shall look forward very much to reading your book when it eventually (if ever) comes out.'

'Thank you,' gulped Quakke inclining his head slightly and blowing another cloud of smoke, intentional this time, at Missmuch.

Missmuch pretended not to notice. He had now put on his best 'fade-out' smile which looked to have come from the same set as those rubber noses to be found in joke-shops. He felt that once again he had fulfilled his duty of exposing to the great British public the dissembling incompetence of those in high places.

As for the blonde lady in the front row she struck anew her mock Churchillian pose as a stimulating burst of Vivaldi brought the programme to its conclusion and when she appeared thus in the middle of the producer's screen he rapidly switched to another camera. This action was not rapid enough however to prevent a few thousand viewers ringing in to say that the Company should really be more careful about whom they invited in future to form the audience for their programmes. Suggestions of qualifications required to attend such an august assembly included references from two people, one of whom should be a J.P, a minimum age limit of fifty, a public school education, and two years in the army.

– – –

'So that's that Quakke chappie,' guffawed Titus Lastick turning off the television set with one hand and with the other throwing a gulp of whisky down his thick gullet. 'Must say he doesn't impress me over much. Like a lot of these American trick-cyclists. All talk if you ask me.'

No one had. He had spoken as though he had watched the programme with a mind open to be impressed whereas the contrary was true. He had taken one look at Hymer's bald head and thick glasses and summed him up at once as typical of his race – loud-mouthed and inarticulate simultaneously, a massive threat to the purity of the English language, probably loaded and working for amusement, frequenting third class musicals and cavorting with bunny-girls in his spare time, to be tolerated if there were dollars to be got out of him, but generally to be despised. Then he had spent the rest of the programme looking for confirmation of his hypothesis which not surprisingly came with abundant regularity.

'I suppose that brazen female in the front row was his wife. Ought never to have taken her along if she was going to make an indecent display of herself. Still I suppose she took him along. Looks the type. Can't imagine for a minute who suggested putting the fellow on the programme anyway.'

Lucy blushed slightly. It happened that one or two of her ex-lovers had been television producers, among them, the producer of "Tête à tête". Still, if he had a suggestion made to him it was up to him whether he took it up or not. It was his responsibility. The fact that he had been trying for a long time to get back into Lucy's favour was neither here nor there. This was the reasoning Mrs Lastick used to absolve herself from any blame in the catastrophe. As we have seen she had no head for abstract ideas, but in the little intricacies of personal relationships she had a certain amount of facility. After all, she thought, the programme might have been a failure, but Hymer seemed a nice man and if she played her cards right she would at least secure the gratitude and trust of Irma Quakke.

'No conscience these chaps.' It was all part of the conversation which had been going on as a background accompaniment to Lucy's thoughts. 'Going round putting ideas into the heads of the young, Not surprising they show such selfishness and lack of public and patriotic feeling. If I had my way fellows like that wouldn't even get a living.'

'Well I do think that awful Mr Missmuch was very nasty to him,' put in Lucy.

'Eh? What? Well, can't say I like these interview chaps much either, but they only do what they're paid to do. Get at the truth eh? If the fellow on the other end can't stand up to him that's his lookout.'

'If you say so, dear.'

'Well I do say so. You always were a bit of a lightweight Lucy.' He puffed importantly at his cigar, priding himself on having demolished his wife's argument. 'Yes, the truth. Don't hear much about that nowadays from these namby pamby soap-box philosophers. Give 'em a factory or two to run, and we'd soon see what brains they have. All theory that's their trouble, all theory.'

'By the way darling,' interrupted Lucy, 'the Turners rang up this afternoon while you were out at golf to say they couldn't come next Saturday, and I was wondering...'

'Hmph. You want to invite that Quakke fellow I'll be bound and that gawky blonde wife of his. Shouldn't be surprised if you didn't get him on television yourself. You always were one of those arty crafty types. Oh well, please yourself, but don't expect me to make high-falutin remarks about the permissive society or go about in topless trousers or whatever the things are they wear. You know what I think about it all. If youngsters don't behave 'emselves they want their bottoms tanning. Only be too pleased to oblige myself but I'm getting on a bit.'

Lastick laughed at his own stalwartness and began to stroke his grey moustache with a thoughtful finger. He was a handsome figure of a man, as indeed was often said in the circles in which he moved. He admired himself for a few minutes in the large gilt wall mirror, took another gulp of whisky and finally expressed his thoughts aloud. 'Can't pretend to understand what you see in these fellows.' He said it as though he were expressing the very height of incomprehensibility.

Having given his judgement he lowered himself carefully into his wing chair and started to think about his next million.

What Lucy had seen in Titus was quite clear. She had looked deep into his eyes, verified that his retina was composed of share certificates and banknotes and fallen in love with him at first insight. After all marriage was security. Sex was a totally unrelated subject. She had never been short of sexual adventure before she married Titus and she had not gone short of it since. Nor did she anticipate a shortage in the foreseeable future. If her sex life had been one of her husband's companies he would, she felt, have been delighted by its solvency. Titus' money, of course, and his position had enabled her to meet men she might otherwise never have come across and the fibre magnate was not too worried about what she got up to in her spare time. As he said, he had married after the death of his first wife to have a bit of decoration about the place (Lucy was certainly that) and he was too old to be jealous. Like her he had made a business arrangement. Not that he didn't take advantage of his conjugal rights. He had held the reputation in his youth of being a bit of a ram and when the fancy took him he could still be a reasonable performer. If only he wouldn't insist on keeping his pyjamas on. It was so Victorian.

Satisfied with his projects, Titus Lastick got to his feet, stretched his arms, yawned and said 'Watching that American fellow has made me feel quite tired. What say we have an early night?'

'Certainly darling,' replied his devoted wife. 'I'll go and get your clean pyjamas.'

— — —

The legendary Nathalie Weinburger once said that love is the expression of its own anticipation. Even Hymer Quakke, who normally curled up into a ball at the merest glimpse of one of her equally legendary hats appearing through the doorway, appreciated this dictum.

It was doubtless with some such sentiment in mind at any rate that Irma, on returning with her husband from the television show which was destined to become as legendary as Nathalie Weinburger herself (or one of her hats), displayed to Hymer every possible endearment. They were settled snugly on the sofa, drinking Scotch with ice but no water, and Irma was reading to him from a paperback version of the 'Kama Sutra', a fact which, with his sound psychological training, Hymer recognised as a prelude to one of her "specials".

She had developed over the years a repertoire of these "specials" which she regarded as necessary to modern, sophisticated nuptial encounters, the sort which all the reputable manuals of the marriage art said were absolutely indispensable in maintaining the magic of each partner for the other.

She had chosen, although she was as yet unaware of her choice, from the one hundred and two varieties employing ice, pickled gherkins, rubber ducks, and orange peel dipped in beef dripping, a particularly potent form of titillation she called "Goosey Goosey".

She stretched out seductively on the sofa letting the last of her Scotch trickle down over her tonsils and raising her hips in a manner she considered to be erotic.

'Hymie darling,' she said huskily in the time honoured tradition of the vamp. 'I'm going to bed now. You won't be long, will you?' With a quick grab at the psycho-anthropoid sociologist's crotch she leapt upstairs.

'You won't be long, will you?' she had said. That meant give me a little time. Quakke was in no particular hurry to go to bed in any case. It was a bad sign, he concluded. She hadn't mentioned Nathalie Weinburger once. He drank his Scotch lazily, crunched the small bits of ice that were left in the glass, then reached for the bottle and poured himself a treble. No, better make it a quadruple. He needed it because of what had gone before and what was to come. He looked, as it were, backward to bedtime with a mixture of gratitude and awe, not to say trepidation. He would never know until the very last minute what was in store for him.

At length, that is to say, two more quadruple Scotches later, putting his glass down resolutely on the dark oak table, he went through his usual bedtime ritual. First he read his Bible, taking care not to pick too long a passage, for it was something of a chore, nor too short a passage, lest he should seem irreverent. Having found one which suited him he read it through, reflected on it for a moment, then completely forgot it. Next he closed the piano lid and locked it, hiding the key in a huge Ming style vase in which he would get his hand stuck next morning trying to retrieve the key. Finally he did ten press-ups, wishing he hadn't drunk so much whisky, bolted the outside doors, extinguished the downstairs lights and went unwillingly upstairs to bed and...that part of it was pure mystery.

He lingered in the bathroom too, taking a warm then a cold shower, a combination he had heard was good for rheumatism from which he never suffered. What had that fellow been on about on television? Could he have made a complete fool of himself? He had not said much, but then that for most people would create a bad impression. Irma had thought it was great, but then she always did. The intellectual life was frankly fatiguing. Perhaps he should have followed his father's advice, and run for Congress. Was he so far ahead of sociological thinking that no one understood him or was he just a bungle-head who couldn't see his own limitations? He came to no great conclusion, but it is just possible that his reflections in the shower that night were significant.

He dried himself and discovered he had left his glasses on in the shower and they were dripping wet. He took them off, had another drying session and put them on again. He sprinkled cologne liberally all over his body, not forgetting behind his ears, then enveloped himself in a fleecy white bathrobe which tied with a rope-like sash. It had been a present from Irma on his forty-second birthday.

'If only I could have another go at that Missmuch fellah I'd show him a thing or two,' he thought, rubbing vigorously at his gums with the toothbrush, so vigorously that they bled profusely and he had to toss tumbler after tumbler full of water around his mouth to staunch the flow.

'Oh well, what the hell, I wonder what she's up to tonight,' he said to himself as he pulled the cord which put out the bathroom light and padded noisily across the thickly carpeted landing to the master bedroom.

The room as he expected was in complete darkness. It was all part of the mystery. Irma saw herself as some kind of oriental seductress rising from the depths of the dark temple of love to draw men to their death, Salaambo setting the hearts of Carthage a throbbing.

Doctor Quakke had no sooner shed his bathrobe and stretched out beside her with a grunt of relief than Irma pulled him on top of her moaning like a cheap tart. 'If only she'd stop acting,' Quakke thought, 'she could be really something. Yes, really something.'

She teased an erection from him, rubbing her groin against it until he felt quite sore, and finally impaled herself on him and began to bounce violently, shouting the while various words of encouragement such as "ride me cowboy" or "come on, baby, sock it to me" together with other unmentionable pieces of advice. Then when she felt he ought to be coming she drew skilfully from beneath the pillow a large goose quill and with the feather end of it began to tickle his scrotum. He collapsed in a paroxysm of laughter and tears and like the Biblical Onan, but for less wicked and more urgent and understandable reasons, he spilt his seed on the ground.

Chapter Three

'The march starts here, Trafalgar Square, where I shall, of course, address the meeting with a few well chosen words.' Those who were acquainted with Kronos knew that he was not exaggerating. 'It ends here at number ten Downing Street where I personally shall deliver the petition to the temporary occupant or his minions. All the necessary publicity has been gone into, I have invited any notable people who have an interest in the cause, and we can confidently expect a good turnout. You two, of course, will keep an eye on the proceedings and see that nothing untoward happens. I shall march up front with the celebrities. That I trust is all. Oh, the police have been informed, and Kaki, what about the banners?'

'There will be ten to a dozen banners with various slogans. They are at present in the next room.' The half-caste girl sprawling naked on the mock-leather studio couch which together with an old half-polished table and three upright chairs formed all the furniture of the basement of number thirteen Bullugly Road, gestured through the open door as if to add unnecessary point to her remark. She closed her eyes and appeared to be asleep.

'Good,' snapped Kronos. 'Any questions?'

The third member of the group slumped pensively across the map, his long blonde hair sweeping the vault of Marble Arch, said nothing. He was watching a small fly which had lighted on the map and was quite fearlessly doing a round tour of London. Logos seemed to be guiding it with his tongue which moved from corner to corner of his wide mouth.

'I said "Any questions?", Logos.' Kronos did not make a habit of repeating himself and the words coming from the back of his throat sounded strange even to him. He banged the table forcibly, but with obvious control, so that the fly took off and the blonde hair stopped its operations.

Logos looked up and there were daggers in his eyes. He had heard the question the first time.

'What about...you know?' he said with some embarrassment like a schoolboy caught smoking in the lavatories. Then his tongue stuck out awkwardly between his teeth and when it returned to its proper resting place it was to allow a wide grin to slash its way across his face.

Kronos did not share his mirth. He drew silently on his Havana cigar and said with a composure and restraint unusual in one of his age, 'Wait, my dear Logos, wait and be silent. Let the forces of time and communication work on you. Have you not been with us long enough to know the proper way? If anything is communicated to you, you will make a sign to me. I shall reply in the normal way. Kaki will do the same.'

Kaki smiled, her eyes still closed.

'Meanwhile,' emphasized Kronos, repeating himself for the second time in a matter of minutes, as if afraid Logos might forget, 'wait and be silent.'

Logos looked mildly rebuked. He stared for a moment across the table at his handsome associate and admitted superior in whose dark eyes he could see nothing but darker and deeper eyes as though he were looking through a telescope back to front. Kronos' face registered no emotion whatsoever.

A silence.

The fly had returned and was crawling negligently along the Mall. Quick as lightning Logos gripped it between two chubby fingers and crushed it, wiping his fingers in his hair, as a grin again lit up his face. Kronos rose slowly and deliberately from his chair and struck the blonde youth three times across the face with the back of his hand.

' You bloody fool, you bloody fool,' he said softly and for the third time he repeated himself. 'You'll spoil everything.' It was said with the force of a prediction rather than a fear. Then he took Logos in his arms, and kissed him, passionately, as a lover.

'Now let us make our trinity.'

The two men undressed. Kaki vacated her position on the couch and was replaced by Kronos who lay flat on his back with his legs straight and together. Kaki straddled him, wriggled until she found the right position, then she too lay flat. Logos, pivoting on her buttocks, made the third, and in this unlikely posture, like some grotesque sandwich of naked flesh, they fell asleep.

After so many goings to bed it would have been nice to have a breakfast scene. Unfortunately Ernest Mann never took breakfast on Sundays, thereby violating his precept which stood good for the rest of the week that everybody should start the day with a good meal. On Sundays he remembered those who could not and confined himself to a cup of black coffee taken in the study as he prepared his Sermon. It was thus that he occupied the time between Communion and lunch.

It was said by the congregation of St Bountiful's that Mann's sermons displayed great courage and conviction, by which they meant they had great difficulty understanding his reasoning and that they themselves would never have dared to stand up in a public place and declaim such nonsense. Whether or not their judgement was accurate is a matter of opinion.

He had got to the rehearsal and correction stage when, collar askew, brow hot and sweaty, and heart thudding resoundingly against his clerical vest, he would confide the thoughts, which had earned him a fourth in theology, to an obscene wood inkstand which the last occupant of the vicarage had brought back from a mission to the Congo and which to say the least was more receptive than his normal congregation.

'...So, if I am, there is no doubt that God exists. (Pause for effect). And if God exists, there is no need to fear. "For it is written, He shall give His angels charge over thee, to keep thee. And in their hands they shall bear thee up lest at any time thou dash thy foot against a stone." The next verse of St Luke came immediately to mind as he read – "And Jesus answering, said unto him, It is said, Thou shalt not tempt the Lord thy God." Nevertheless he pressed on.

'In a world where fear and violence play an ever increasing role, this message must inevitably have more importance for us. When we see corruption all around us should we not feel more needful of the guiding hand of the Angel (Better make it plural) – of the Angels when we are at any time likely... (No, "in danger of" sounds better. Start that bit again.) ...should we not feel more needful of the guiding hand of the Angels...'

There was a knock at the thick eighteenth century door and Mann was rather relieved to see peeping round it, not an Angel, but a twentieth century Martha, with round face and white hair, who had come to announce that lunch was ready. The announcement was unnecessary as Mann had detected a smell of roast beef emanating from the dining room next door when he was about to launch a particularly violent tirade against the evils of the flesh. He thanked his wife however and promised to join her presently when his revision was complete.

'...when we are at any time in danger of dashing our feet against a stone. And if this were to be my very last sermon, I should still put my charge in God to be there at the end to justify and claim the fruits of my existence.'

It was in a mood of self-congratulation, not far from the sin of pride, he told himself quickly, that Mann opened the door of his study once more and came into the dining room. Not one of his worst efforts anyway, he compromised.

As he sat down to carve, his wife said:

'You haven't forgotten that demonstration, dear? You know you promised Lucy last week?'

'No I haven't forgotten,' replied Mann with something like resignation, 'although I must admit I don't like getting involved with these people. The young man should never have got into the situation. On the other hand one does feel that nowadays the Church should be involved in political questions especially when the individual appears to be fighting a losing battle all round for his freedom.'

A young Communist agitator had been convicted and imprisoned for an assault on a well known MP's daughter, although the evidence had been far from sound. Several appeals had been made, but it was felt in some circles that the Prime Minister, who had been more than embarrassed by recent demonstrations organised by the youth, was for a time at least, restraining the Home Secretary's hand. The present demonstration was intended to bring to a head the torrent of feeling which had been aroused by what people all over the country and especially the young considered an overt piece of rough justice.

At quarter to three the familiar white Cadillac pulled up in the vicarage drive. The sparrows, remembering the last occasion, had decided to take their Sunday afternoon nap in the back garden so there was no danger of British wildlife being in any way depleted as the gravel groaned under the weight of the car.

Mann, who could hardly have been unaware of their presence, was at the front door before anyone could get out of the car. Irma and Hymer had collected Lucy on their way to the vicarage to save them having to use two cars. Theirs, as the Quakkes said, had plenty of room for everybody.

'Ernest, you've met Irma, I think. This, of course, is Hymer Quakke.' Lucy was performing a social function she had now brought to a fine art, having at least as many ways of introducing people as her American equivalent had 'specials'.

'So you're in this business too, Quakke,' said Mann with furious jollity, having responded to the introduction with his usual hand shake.

'Well, yeah, I guess..'

'Such a good opportunity of studying one of these demos first hand. We simply had to come along,' put in the irrepressible Mrs Quakke.

'I guess,' Hymer continued, 'I'm not old enough to reply for myself.' It was perhaps the first real sign.

Ernest Mann did not know what to say. Lucy, who did, said quickly.

'Come on, we haven't much time to spare. Get in everybody.'

And the journey to London was passed in a none too comfortable silence.

– – –

They parked the car as near as possible to their destination, Ernest Mann remarked, enjoying one of his familiar theological jokes, but that still meant a longish walk before they arrived at Trafalgar Square.

The square, as indeed they had expected, was packed. Nelson, who must by now have had enough of these unorthodox brawling parties, no doubt turned his blind eye on the situation. Three of the lions were being mounted and ridden in a way that being real they would certainly not have tolerated. The fourth, having been too recently occupied by a family of pigeons, preserved thereby his peace if not his dignity. The fountain was amply justifying Archimedes' principle and appeared to be performing a useful cleansing function on a sizeable cohort of young people, many of whom in appearance, were in need of its ministrations. One young lady, perhaps to compensate for the lack of sculpture created by the interment of Landseer's Lions beneath swarms of uncouth bodies, had taken off her clothes and struck a pose, which although not entirely Classical, had nevertheless some claim to beauty. Natural beauty being essentially ephemeral, she was forcibly removed in an act of vandalism, second only to the rape of the Elgin marbles, by the gentlemen of the Metropolitan Police.

Irma almost forgot her husband's snub in the maelstrom of MPs, elderly dons, clergymen, and the ebullient, effervescent young which greeted them as they came to the Square proper. It was as though the whole of the square was one great flower-bed with the bright blooms of youth set off against the more sober background of experience, the one sprung from the other as flowers from the ground. On the observer it had an almost hypnotic effect and in the participant it created an impression that one was deliriously treading grapes and simultaneously drinking the wine.

Some people near the fountain had brought a guitar and were singing with more gusto than melody the war cry of the Civil Rights movement. 'We shall overcome some day,' Its sentiment contrasted strangely with the apparent exuberance and impatience of the singers for whom some day was a great deal too late. Others had brought large banners lavishly painted and bearing bold slogans, ranging from the very simple 'Free Tomkins now' to the provocative 'Who really dun it?', the imperative 'Hands off Tomkins', and the philosophical 'What price justice now?'

The quartet moved towards the platform where a very suave looking young man, dark and handsome with the hint of the Jew about his features, was discussing some detail of the march with an olive skinned girl in a white see-through mini dress and a long blonde haired youth in a purple suit with flared trouser bottoms, at the same time encouraging the adding of more signatures to his list. A new contingent of protesters had arrived to add their names. They were singing and smelt strongly of drink. One had a banner saying 'Free Tommy the Red'.

The dark man looked at them without speaking for a few minutes as they scrawled illegibly at the bottom of the paper he was holding with a thick black felt pen. Then he said:

'We welcome your support, of course, but I'm sure I don't need to remind you that this is a peaceful demonstration, and that if you attract attention to yourselves you will do so to us likewise, and the interests of the person we are trying to help will hardly be served.'

'Okay, mate. Okay,' said the one with the black droopy moustache and the frizzy hair who appeared to be the leader. Then they went away singing louder than ever and shouting 'Sieg Heil'.

'There are always some, the scavengers of any demonstration, who use it for their own ends.' The dark young man was turning towards Lucy. A smile began to cut across the blonde youth's face. Kronos gave him a look, then turned again.

'Glad you could come, Lucy.' He kissed her full on the mouth to the embarrassment of Mann who pretended the while to be interested in Nelson. 'It's been a long time.'

'Yes, it has, but I've really been terribly busy. You know how things pile up on one,' laughed Lucy.

'Indeed,' agreed Kronos.

Lucy was speaking again. 'When you rang me and asked me to bring some people along, Julian, I had simply no idea who. Then I thought well, why not some one from my own back yard, as it were? And here they are. In the red corner, the Rev. Mann...'

'Well I don't know about the red bit,' muttered Mann, 'but how do you do anyway.' He extended his hand and was surprised how cold the other's was.

'And in the blue corner,' continued Lucy, 'Dr Quakke and Mrs Quakke.'

'Hi,' beamed Irma. 'Call me Irma.'

'How do you do,' whispered Quakke. 'Call me Quakke,' he said more loudly.

'Where on earth has he gotten his sense of humour from?' wondered Irma, becoming aware of her husband's previous shortcomings all at once, and growing more and more disturbed.

'And over here,' pointed Julian beckoning Kaki and Logos to come closer, 'we have Julie and Fritz.'

The handshaking began again.

'Dr Quakke,' said Lucy, 'is over here to write a book on the Permissive Society.'

'How interesting,' thought Julian for a moment, then turned towards his companions. Fritz of the long blonde hair had taken out a silver cigarette case. He offered it first to Mann. Lucy thought this showed a distinct lack of etiquette.

'No thank you. I don't smoke,' Mann mumbled with a wave of the hand.

Fritz went round the whole group in turn. Quakke already had his meerschaum going full speed ahead so Irma was the last.

'No, look,' butted in Julian, brushing aside the cigarette case as it reached Irma, 'you've only got five left.' And he proffered a full packet of Lucky Strike.

'Thanks,' breathed Irma as Julian lit the cigarette.

Fritz and Julie smiled. A bargain had been made.

'I do believe that boy fancies me,' mused Irma.

– – –

Julian went on to the platform and began to say his few well chosen words.

'Ladies and gentlemen, others,' he said, eyeing the late comers who had gravitated towards the fountain and were bathing their feet. 'You all know why you are here. I have here a petition bearing more than thirty thousand signatures.' He waved a sheaf of papers which looked almost like a wad of notes. 'It asks for an immediate review of the whole Tomkins situation. When this petition reaches Downing Street and the effect of our protest is felt I am confident that that is exactly what will happen. One more word. This is a peaceful demonstration. We shall march in orderly fashion and we shall disband likewise. I shall have no sympathy whatsoever with anyone who makes trouble for himself with the police. Thank you.'

'Hear, hear,' shouted Mann in spite of his usual reserve. He was beginning to enjoy this. Taken with his successful sermon this was really a very good day. Julian looked down at the little figure with the large spectacles perched on the end of his enormous nose, the wide mouth, the chin which protruded but ended flat as though it were a potato which had had a bad piece sliced off it. He looked at the skinny neck where all the veins and sinews stood out and which disappeared into the clerical collar like a snake into a basket. He smiled at him.

Mann smiled back. 'Yes, this really was a beautiful day.'

With Julian and the quartet at its head the procession marched off, Julie and Fritz slipping quietly into the ranks.

Chapter Four

'I must say quite frankly that I was surprised,' Ernest confided to Titus Lastick. 'I had expected a great deal of violence and unruliness.'

It was the Saturday following Mann's weekend of spiritual and political triumph.

'You mean you were disappointed,' laughed Lastick.

'On the contrary, it was most gratifying to see the young behaving in such a responsible and dignified...'

'It's not my idea of dignity and responsibility to go on one of those marches, demos, sit-downs, or whatever you call them.'

Ernest was quick to spring to his own defence although the tactical thing to do would have been to change the subject. 'But you must admit, Titus,' he was saying, 'there are certain perfectly legitimate ways of protesting about the erosion of certain principles.' He had deliberately left it vague. ' This is still fundamentally a free society, you know.'

'Free be damned,' exploded Lastick going very red in the face, almost the colour of the claret he was drinking. 'I've got nothing out of this world, Ernest, that I haven't paid for, and I don't just mean with money. You know how I started with nothing, worked my way up by my own toil or sweat.' He was making a passable imitation of the process as though a part of his past had been suggested to him.

'Yes, of course.' Mann did not want to hear all that again. 'What I really meant was that there are some things we see as our rights as citizens of a particular country or of the world if you like, and we are quite right in protesting when we think they are being violated, whether with relation to ourselves or to other people. We were perfectly justified in demonstrating (he said this although he had not personally done so) against the sale of arms to South Africa because we believed that thereby the rights of the black South Africans to enjoy certain standards of living, which we take for granted in this country, and to participate in the running of their own affairs, might be prejudiced.'

'If you're talking about rights...' Lastick was growing a deeper and deeper shade of purple. It was not his habit to be contradicted, either by Mann or anybody else '...what about the right of privacy, the right to get on with one's own business without anybody else poking their nose into it. If a South African wants to buy guns from me, it's his affair what he does with them. If he chooses to go and shoot a few blacks, what the hell. There are enough of the bastards, and so long as he doesn't interfere with me I'm quite prepared to let him alone. I'm surprised at you, Ernest. I thought you were a steady sensible type. Seems you've been converted to the other side by all these emotional demonstrations.'

'Well, it was only one,' said Mann, not prepared to continue the subject. 'Whatever else you might say about it,' he concluded, 'I must say I was impressed by the way that young fellow Julian handled the whole affair.'

'Ah yes,' grunted Lastick, '...advertising man. One of Lucy's old friends. I gather she's invited him here tonight.'

'In that case I shall look forward to meeting him again.'

'Here, have another drink,' said Lastick gruffly, because he felt he needed one himself.

– – –

A loud peal of laughter announced the arrival of the Quakkes. Irma, noted Mann, looked rather attractive for her age even though there was a suggestion of mutton dressed as lamb in her pale blue mini-dress and the white shoes with the extravagant gilt buckles.

Greetings were exchanged, drinks poured, Lastick not missing the opportunity of offering himself another.

'You must tell Titus all about your book, Hymer,' teased Lucy seeing the effect it had on her husband,

'Well, look, if you don't mind, Mr Lastick, I'd rather not talk about it at the moment. It's er going through a crisis and it would be better to leave the subject completely alone for a few days, I guess.'

'Oh,' said Irma.

'Call me Titus,' said Lastick, pouring himself another drink.

— — —

Several other people arrived, and the party, as they say, had begun to get going. The usual small talk developed, punctuated here and there by snap judgements on political questions, art, and the races. Doreen Farnaby's girl had just become engaged, Peter Broadhurst was convincing Lastick of the value of holdings in Consolidated tyres, Lucy's flower arrangements were much admired, they were all pleased to see the Tories back in except the television producer who thought that the whole country had been put back ten years and, secretly, that Lucy's dress was beautiful, and what was in it even more beautiful. Simon Garfield had won three thousand at Ascot the week before just by following horses whose names had begun with the same letter as the names of childhood sweethearts. It had caused his wife to sulk for a few days but she had a completely new outfit for the autumn, and a new mini-car out of it.

At half past ten Lucy made herself heard above the confused chatter through which could be occasionally heard a blurred voice saying ' Have another one, old boy.'

'If you would like to come into the dining room, the buffet is all ready. Just help yourselves everybody.'

At a quarter to eleven the door bell rang. Lucy went and found Julian, Julie and Fritz standing outside.

'Sorry we're late,' said the spokesman. 'We had a puncture about a mile back. And the damned spare wheel was at home.' He kissed Lucy.

'Steady on,' she said, by no means reprovingly. 'My husband lives here, you know. Come in anyway. We've just started eating.'

The three were ushered into the dining room where they renewed old acquaintances and made new ones. They took a plate each and began to circulate. Fritz was taken off by Lucy to meet the television producer who was still more interested in sex than television or the government although he kept on stoically talking about both. Julie, on the other hand, was quickly pounced upon by Titus Lastick who had drunk enough to forget his colour prejudice and was offering to show her the garden. Perhaps it should be said in mitigation that the lights in the room were deliberately not very bright and Julie might easily be thought to have spent the last month in the Bahamas and acquired a superb tan, most of which was evident.

Julian gravitated towards the corner where Irma Quakke and Ernest Mann were sitting together on the sofa.

'Pity your poor wife couldn't come, Ernest,' Irma was saying as Julian came within earshot. 'She would really have enjoyed herself.'

'Yesh, it is rather,' replied Mann, stopping a gherkin halfway to his mouth. 'But she had promised to go and see an old friend of hers this weekend. She was most disappointed of course. We do like these little get togethers in the parish. Such a pleasant way of getting to know people.' He was beginning to feel the influence of these first drinks which had come to him rather quicker than he had anticipated. What had he been saying in his last sermon about the evils of the flesh? Well never mind that now, he thought, as his eyes strayed to the little white triangle under the hem of Irma's dress.

'And how will you look after yourself all by your poor little self tomorrow with a sermon to prepare and everything?' Since Hymie was behaving in such a queer fashion she would have to make her own arrangements.

'Oh don't worry about that,' spluttered Mann through a celery biscuit, sensing the danger and quick to try and put himself out of temptation's reach. 'That's all taken care of. There is a very good soul from the village who helps Letitia out sometimes and she has very kindly offered to come and prepare meals for me.'

'Easier than we thought,' breathed Julian to himself as he glanced across at Fritz who was showing the television producer his favourite trick of making his long hair stand absolutely stiff, so that it could even be broken off.

He pulled up a chair and sat opposite the couple. Mann made to get up and extend his hand, but Irma stopped him.

'Oh Ernest,' she drawled, 'don't stand on ceremony. I'm sure Julian doesn't mind. Give your arse a rest.'

'Well really,' thought Mann, 'but then I suppose there might be something to be said for the woman's overwhelming sincerity. We must move with the times after all. We must move with the times.'

'I do hope I'm not interrupting anything,' said Julian to Irma, who up to that moment, strange as it may seem, had never thought of it in that way. 'One does hear so much these days about chance meetings at parties. Even the clergy, one hears, are not immune to the evils of the flesh.'

Mann took this conversation of Julian's as he thought it was intended, frivolously, but at the last words he started. Why had this young man used the very same words he had reminded himself of only a few minutes ago and which he had used in a sermon only a week ago? He began to choke on a small pickled onion.

'Say, are you alright?' said Irma, giving the reverend gentleman a resounding slap on the back.

'I fear not the disease but thy cure,' he thought to himself as he breathed freely again.

'Yesh, yesh,' he laughed the whole thing off. He really mustn't take so much notice of any little thing people said to him. He must make a conscious effort of will to resist.

Julian felt in his jacket pocket and took out a packet of cigarettes. He opened them first to Irma, who thanked him and took one, and then to Ernest. 'Here, have one of these, they'll help to steady your nerves.' He spoke with such coolness that Mann was not offended.

'Well, I don't normally…'

'Go on, Ernest. It is a party after all.' It was Irma again.

'Well, thank you very much, er, Julian, isn't it?'

'Say no more,' said Julian. He put a cigarette in his mouth then lit all three.

Mann looked as though he would begin coughing again, but he seemed to have steadied and was looking at the other two with a glazed expression that was made all the more literal by his large spectacles and the small eyes which blinked behind them. The left eye was slightly red and watery at the corner from the smoke.

'It's funny. I'm quite enjoying this,' said the clergyman. The last time he had smoked had been when he was fourteen in the old school lavatory and he had been caught. His buttocks contracted slightly at the memory. It was a perfectly normal cigarette but he couldn't get the idea out of his mind that it might be drugged. 'Absurd,' said the resistant will.

There was absolutely no reason for his belief, yet he was growing uncomfortably warm. If he had been able to come out of himself he would have realised that everyone was suffering from the heat. Lucy had just opened the window wider, and Fritz's hair was blowing about in the breeze as he told the producer he was a liberal. Lastick had come in with Julie from the garden, yet he looked more purple and hot than ever, although he had not smoked for a quarter of an hour. All this however passed unnoticed by Mann.

He took another drag at the cigarette, which was only half-smoked. It was another effort to convince himself that nothing was wrong. The more he tried to shake off the idea that the cigarette was drugged, the more he felt its effects on him, the more deeply the idea rooted itself in his brain, gnawing at it with monotonous regularity so that he had the bizarre sensation that he had a headache not near the surface but deep down inside.

Irma and Julian appeared to have been carrying on a conversation the whole time.

Suddenly Mann became conscious of them again.

'I must say I find these American cigarettes very stimulating, don't you Mrs Quakke?'

'Well, as far as I'm concerned, one likes what one is used to.'

'The only drawback, of course, is the expense. Still, one must have some pleasures, don't you agree, Mann?'

'Oh yes, of course.' He was only saying that to try and persuade him that there was nothing wrong with the cigarettes, thought Ernest. In fact nothing could have been further from the truth.

'After all,' Julian continued, 'the Angels are watching over us lest we dash our foot against a stone.'

'Oh, indeed.' That sermon again, the one he had said might be his last. How on earth? If he had thought clearly he would have asked Julian where he had heard the expression and might have found out that his congregation the previous Sunday had been larger by one, but he didn't. A further seed of panic began to put roots into his brain.

'Would you like another drink?' Irma's raucous voice was suddenly so soothing. 'Now why don't I go and get us all one?'

'Yes, that would be nice,' said Mann. He had already had enough but wanted something to take away the taste of the cigarette he had just finished and resolutely stubbed out in the ash tray.

'You don't look very well, Mann,' said Julian when Irma had gone. 'Can I do anything for you?'

'No, dear boy, no, I'm perfectly alright.'

Irma came back with the drinks. Ernest drank his and felt slightly better. He saw things clearly. The dark man opposite had drugged him some woman and if he were not really resolute...

'If you two will excuse me, I must circulate a bit more. Don't do anything I wouldn't do.'

Julian took his half-full glass and went to talk to Fritz and the television producer.

'Such a nice man, don't you think?' Irma giggled.

'Oh, yes indeed,' said Ernest.

'I'm sure he has some very trendy friends we could introduce to Hymie. It would be so useful for his book. I do think these young people are so much freer than we were. Hymie says it's got something to do with their regressive post-natalism or something.'

'Indeed,' said Ernest. He was obsessed with his second idea now. He really would do something very silly unless...

'I mean you and I were so well repressed when we were their age, and even now we don't really know how to go about things, we need looking after the whole time, especially you poor weak men.'

She put an arm around Mann.

'Say honey, wouldn't you like to take a walk around the garden...?'

'I believe I would,' said Mann meekly.

They carved a way through masses of laughing, chattering, drinking bodies unnoticed except by three people who seemed to have drunk less than everyone else and seemed therefore to be in command of their faculties. As Kronos said, ' No one needs tobacco or alcohol when his mind is perfectly sound.'

Irma's hand felt strangely comforting to Mann. He had never had such a feeling before in his life. He was dizzy, but was surprised to find it was not unpleasant. They strolled down to the summer house at the bottom of the dark garden. It seemed to Mann that he was falling into a deep black pit where time had no meaning and space was infinite. The harder he tried to stop himself falling, the more rapidly he tumbled downwards. But he was not anxious or afraid. He felt intensely relieved.

He was unconscious of how he got home to the vicarage. In fact, to all appearances he had been perfectly normal and cheerful when the Quakkes dropped him off there. He had gone up to bed, moved the window to get some fresh air.

He was found that morning lying flat on his back on the lawn with a distinctly beatific expression on his face, and who was to say that his Angels had not been there at the last?

– – –

The general surprise at the death of such an eminent citizen of Tolbridge was not shared, as might indeed be imagined, by the three members of the Association for Recreational Euthanasia, which already had on its record books twenty or so such suicides.

The method of ARE will be familiar enough by now, for it not to need elaboration. Suffice it to say, if any person were to be suspected of being instrumental in the death of the unfortunate victim, it would not be Kronos, Logos, or Kaki. Usually there was no suspicion at all, except perhaps in the mind of someone who, under the influence of suggestion from one of the trio, might have become the unwilling agent of their will. Even so, persons such as this would naturally have good reason to keep quiet.

The Sunday evening sun had just sunk low enough to penetrate the dirt-spattered windows of the basement flat and to play shimmering games with the beautiful bronze flesh of the girl on the black couch. She was staring with childish amusement at the flames licking the chimney of the old Victorian fireplace as Logos fed it with pieces of wood and cardboard on which large letters were still distinguishable.

A deep-eyed man was playing Patience with tiny cards on the worn table, cheating so that the game always came out. He saw no point whatsoever in trusting to fickle fortune.

'I must say you handled that very well,' said Logos with evident glee. ' The poor old geezer's probably lying there all in white on his four-poster bed, his missus wailing and gnashing her teeth all over him. Lovely innit?'

'I am not sure I approve of your style,' retorted Kronos. 'Nevertheless, one does feel some satisfaction over a job well done.'

'Ah, you always did talk better than I do,' said Logos ruefully. 'Still it comes to the same thing, don't it? Another success for ARE.'

'Indeed.' Kronos returned to his cards.

'Is that all you're going to say? What's the next move now?'

'Must I always do things for you, Logos?' Kronos put his hands to his head in a gesture of despair. 'I have told you time and time again to use your intuition and imagination rather than that stubborn will of yours. Mann had a will like that, and look what happened to him. You saw instinctively he was a good subject. Why don't you apply your instinct more readily?'

'It's that Quakke woman innit?'

'Right first time. She is intelligent enough for our purpose but not too intelligent. She has an obsessive streak. She has an over developed maternal instinct which seeks to protect anyone who appears to be unable to fend for himself. That's why she married Quakke. She likes to lead him about like a little boy. An interesting one for a psychologist. I wonder he hasn't noticed it. It was this obsession I put a good use to yesterday, so that while seeking to protect dear Ernest, she was the final cause of his destruction, though admittedly not the essential one which lay in himself. She is, as I said, intelligent enough to feel her part in Mann's downfall, and she will dwell on that. She will thus be in a perfectly receptive state for her own death.'

'Yeh, but how do we finish it off this time?' said Logos.

Kronos was becoming bored. 'You tell him, Kaki.'

Kaki stirred on the couch. 'A woman to do a woman's work,' she said sleepily.

'And you,' added Kronos, pointing at Logos, 'will prepare Lucy.'

'Yeh, well, should be interesting anyway,' mused Logos.

Chapter Five

Quakke had started keeping a diary. He had hitherto been that kind of introspective who hesitates to confide his thoughts even to paper, perhaps in fear of the not unlikely event of someone finding it and reading what he had been most careful to conceal. Now, however, he was quite determined to record his reflections for himself, and perhaps becoming vain enough to think they might be of interest to posterity. The essential significance of the step he was taking was that he was prepared to take the risk of the diary being found and perused by Irma.

That Sunday evening when his wife had been prompted by the spirit of compassion or some other anonymous motive to go and commiserate with Mrs Mann, who she felt would appreciate her sympathy, Quakke wrote the following entry in his diary.

'Aim – to know myself, to distinguish what thoughts are my own from those which have been planted in my subconscious by others. To concentrate less on my surroundings and more on my own personality. To develop all the faculties I know I possess and to bring forth those I as yet only suspect. To achieve the sort of independence which is unseen and does not need to prove itself.'

He took up a book which was lying on the felt topped writing table next to his left elbow. His lighter was on his right and his mottled meerschaum directly in front of him on top of his tobacco pouch. Before opening the book he began to smoke. He held the smoke in his mouth for a long time before releasing it. As he focussed on the first page the interval between puffs became less as the smoke gradually and involuntarily measured the speed of his assimilation of words and phrases. He grew conscious of the speed with which the pipe was running away with him and now drew in a breath and held it each time smoke passed from the mouthpiece into his mouth. He began to memorise words, phrases, sentences, then paragraphs, and finished by remembering a whole page.

When he had done this he let out a sigh of satisfaction, put down his pipe on the green felt as he always did with his index finger, took up his pen, and wrote again.

'I shall not head my entries with a date. It is of little consequence to me. I shall make an entry every day and I shall name the day.'

'Sunday'

'Irma has gone out. She seems to believe that she has a mysterious gift for making people happy and she has gone to use it on poor Ernest's wife. She has not realised that sympathy bestowed in the wrong way and at the wrong time can be as heartless as an insult, as cruel as a blow on the head. She will upset Mrs Mann and put her increased grief down to the progressive unbearability of this totally unexpected mourning which has been imposed on her.'

'She (Irma) was quieter than usual, however, and she appeared to be more concerned than she should have been. I shall not try to explain it yet. I shall only confuse myself if I make extravagant guesses on the basis of one observation. I shall wait and say nothing about it. If there is really anything wrong she will tell me. She is quite incapable of keeping up a pretence.'

'For the first time in my life I enjoyed making love to a woman. Perhaps 'love' is the wrong word because love as we normally understand it did not enter into it. I merely allowed my instinct full play. The act was not spoiled for me by the thought that it was my duty. I felt no guilt about betraying Irma. When she makes love to me she employs every possible means to try and arouse my desire, to maintain my pleasure, but it is for herself that she does it, to confirm in her mind the idea that she is the important one. It makes her feel good to think she has been my slave. She must ask me afterwards if I enjoyed it. She must have all the time my devotion to confirm her own. Lucy asked for nothing and was given nothing. No, I am wrong. If she found out Irma would be bound to ask...'

'What could she give you that I could not?'

'And if I were to reply truthfully...'

'Herself. For a moment, for an insignificant time to you perhaps. And I gave myself to her and was able to take it back again. Can you possibly realise what this means to me?'

'She would not be able. If she picked some poor sod up in the gutter, felt sorry for him, and fornicated with him on a park bench, despite his filth, an action which would be entirely in character, she dared not let it rest at that. She would have to seek him out, remind the poor devil of what she owed him, and of what he owed her, even if it took her the rest of her life to find him again.'

A thought came to him but he postponed it. He picked up the pipe, raised the lighter to it, but decided he had no need of it. He threw the lot – pipe, tobacco, lighter – into the waste paper basket, and listened with indefinable pleasure to the metallic rattles as they clattered from the sides and settled dead in the bottom.

'I have not written a word of my book on the Permissive Society for three days. It is possible that I shall not write another. The two pages of my diary I have just written are more important to me, and perhaps to others, than the fifty written by me but composed by Irma.'

Quakke closed the diary and his eyes simultaneously. He remained like that for ten minutes, then he placed the diary in a hidden drawer he had found in the old bureau, and went over to the piano.

– – –

It was not only Hymer Quakke who had been trying to put his thoughts in perspective. His wife too had been doing some hard thinking.

On leaving the cottage, she had not gone straight to the vicarage, but had driven around for half an hour or so., she had not been particularly conscious where. She had controlled the car like a robot.

Why had she tried to keep up a cheerful face before Hymie? It would have been nice to make a clean breast about everything to him. She was sure he would have understood. Still he wouldn't have been very pleased about his wife having it off with another man. Her mind was using the colourful slang Irma took to be indispensable to existence in modern Britain. She had to make the sacrifice and keep it to herself. Suffer alone and in silence. She was making basically a good job of it, and Hymie would never notice. Still with this added to the strange way Hymer was behaving, it really made life bloody unbearable.

She couldn't see any reason for it. After all, he had been perfectly cheerful when... She had heard about old men passing away in the throes of ecstasy with young girls. But not a couple of hours afterwards. That was ridiculous. It could have had nothing whatsoever to do with what she and he... And that was ridiculous too. It seemed too much of a coincidence. "FRAGILE OLD PARSON MAKES LOVE TO YOUNG WOMAN UNDER THE INFLUENCE OF LIQUOR. FILLED WITH REMORSE COMMITS SUICIDE." The headline was rather long, but she could see it in inch high capitals, occupying almost the whole page of one of the popular Sunday newspapers she had taken to reading while the Sunday joint cooked. But she was in the mood for exaggeration. She had even exaggerated the 'young woman' bit. It was true she was well preserved, it was true she was healthy and vigorous, but her mind if not her heart had begun to take on the patterns of middle age. She never went without her afternoon nap now and she had started looking for grey hairs, although she had not yet found one. Oh my God, she was thinking, if this ever got out...'

The shock of the possible future brought her back to the present. She realised she was a good ten miles outside Tolbridge, and she turned resolutely, and made for the vicarage.

– – –

The curtains of all the windows were drawn, those on the ground floor slightly parted, so that Irma was painfully reminded that the episode was not yet closed.

As she waited for the door to be answered, she was trying to think what she would say when there appeared before her on the doorstep the woman whose...

'Yes?' said a plump body whose presence in other circumstances would have been welcoming and reassuring.

The indecision as to what to say was postponed. It was the 'good soul from the village.'

'If you want to see Mrs Mann she's in the sitting room. But if I was you I'd be careful what you said. She isn't really in the best of spirits. Understandably, of course. Dreadful thing. Dreadful thing.'

She was shaking her head. It was a further reminder that she ought not to have come.

'Thank you,' said Irma and followed the woman in.

– – –

Letitia Mann was sitting at one end of a large old fashioned sofa which had certainly occupied its position in the house for many years more than herself. She looked almost impressively small as she used her handkerchief liberally on swollen red eyes which had not been by any means subdued to dryness by her faith and her belief that Ernest was now in the best of all possible worlds. Perhaps she was more preoccupied with the thought that she inhabited the worst without him. She made a silent, but eloquent, gesture to Irma to sit down.

'I can't understand it,' said Letitia Mann. 'I only saw him two days ago and he was perfectly alright, quite happy.' The thought of it made her burst into tears, making her handkerchief an ineffective white sponge.

'I just came to say how sorry I am,' said Irma. 'I mean I just know what you must be feeling. I know how I'd feel if it had been... If there's anything I can do, don't hesitate... Such a tragedy. He seemed perfectly well, well early this morning...' (Better avoid that subject, something said to her.)

'That's what I can't understand. Poor Ernest was so looking forward to this party of Lucy's, although you know he's not, was not, the kind of man to indulge his body in the way some people do.'

'No, I can appreciate that,' Irma winced. Why on earth had she come?

Letitia seemed to be finding breath and comfort now in talking.

'He used to say to me, "We have other pleasures, Letitia, which come from ourselves and our relationships with other people, our helpfulness to each other, besides those artificial stimulants which man has manufactured for himself." Do you see what I mean?'

'Yes, of course, Mrs Mann, I don't know...' What on earth was she going to say? It couldn't do any good.

'There'll be an inquest of course. They won't say anything, but I know he must have been drunk. It's never happened before and I can't understand why he... but I know he must have been. Oh it's horrible. What must the poor man have been thinking? I could have forgiven him, I think, but could he have forgiven himself? That's the question I've been asking myself. Was that it? And yet he seemed somehow to sense something last week when he preached that sermon.'

'It was a marvellous sermon, Mrs Mann.'

'Yes, ironic, isn't it? His best sermon too and he had to go just when he was improving, when...' The handkerchief once again did more than its duty.

'Well, I think I'd better be going now, I just wanted to...'

'No, don't go,' Letitia almost shouted so that Irma fell back with a bump onto the chair. 'I must face up to people.' "Let the dead bury their dead", isn't that what Jesus said? As a matter of fact, I wanted to ask you Mrs Quakke whether you found anything at all unusual in my husband's behaviour...?'

'Well, no, not really,' Irma lied. 'In fact he seemed very happy to tell you the truth.'

'Oh, just what I expected. As I said, the poor dear was drinking, he who couldn't stand it.'

'He didn't appear to drink very much at all.'

'Not for some people, but Ernest wasn't used to it. They say for some the first temptation is the last. I didn't see the significance of the remark until now. Still, I don't suppose I shall feel like this for ever.'

'I guess not,' said Irma, guessing that she might. 'Look I really must be going.'

'Very well. You have your husband to attend to and I mine in our different ways. Thank you for coming. You can rest assured you were able to give me some help, although to be honest when I first saw who it was I was inclined to melt into the floor. If I don't see you again (I shall be leaving as soon as this business is over you see) may I wish you and your husband the happiness Ernest and I shared? If we meet not here we shall meet perchance in Heaven.'

'Perchance,' sighed Irma. 'Goodbye, Mrs Mann. I do hope everything goes alright for you.'

'Goodbye,' said Letitia, already braver.

– – –

'Damned funny business, that's what I call it,' said Lastick putting on his pyjamas. 'Fellow goes home from a party and throws himself out of the window. Reminds me of me army days when chaps went over the top to stop being shelled. Damned funny business. What went on at that party?, that's what I want to know, and him a parson too. Well, it takes all sorts, they say, but I'm damned if I understand 'em. And Ernest, y'know. He was such a stable fellow, though I must say I thought he'd gone potty the way he carried on about that demonstration. Don't suppose you know anything about it, Lucy? After all, it was your party...'

'One can't watch all one's guests all the time darling. In a gathering that size they must keep some secrets to themselves.'

'Hmph,' grunted Titus who had secrets of his own which he saw Lucy might discover. 'Let's leave it at that then. Only hope it doesn't get into the papers. Damned funny business,'

He got clumsily into bed, nearly bouncing out of the other side, reached up to pull the light cord, then sank down again like an angry whale.

When all was dark and quiet Lucy could still hear him muttering between his teeth.

'Damned funny business though.'

– – –

'After hearing all the available evidence,' pronounced the Coroner, 'it is my duty to record a verdict of accidental death. There seems to be no strong indication that the deceased was in any way unhappy or unbalanced. In fact most of those who were in his company on the night in question have asserted the contrary. The pathologist has confirmed that although the unfortunate person had taken some alcohol, he was unlikely to have been made so drunk by it as to be unaware of what he was doing. Nevertheless, a slight diminution of his faculties combined with the awkwardness of the window frame which has been attested to most probably caused him to lose his footing and to hurtle through the window with tragic results. While expressing all possible sympathy with the deceased's wife I feel I should point out that danger lurks in the most innocent places when our property is in a bad state of disrepair.'

Chapter Six

The following is an extract from Quakke's diary.

'Thursday'

'My faculties are improving every single day. I forget almost nothing. I am able to reason clearly about everything. I am able not to read minds but to perceive them. I have not one superstitious habit left. Anyone reading this would by now have convicted me of boastfulness or self-deception. This would be unjust. For the first, in my normal everyday affairs with people I make no claim whatsoever. I am content to rely on the effect of my words or actions, on the keeping of a promise, on a decision based on evaluation of all the factors involved. Why should I, moreover, be satisfied with any but the highest standards for myself?, and having set them firmly in my mind, why should I as a man of no mean ability fail to live up to them? As to the second, I hold there is no man living who does not in some form or another practise it. To inspire it to others is perhaps the gravest mistake of all.'

'Irma has been very subdued this week. It takes extraordinarily little perspicacity to divine the reason. She was involved in some way with poor Mann's death. Her surprise at the result of the inquest was accompanied by not a little relief. She has been so wrapped up in herself she has not noticed changes which have taken place in me. That is completely foreign to her nature. I feel sure that she will tell me soon what I already know, that she and Ernest had an affair, and that she feels responsible for his death. This may be possible, indirectly, but I am certain it is not the whole truth, for which I shall have to wait, although I fear the waiting may be costly.'

'When she reveals to me what went on between her and Mann, I shall say nothing about Lucy and myself. Only guilt or shame is a factor in both, and I have already said I feel neither of them.'

'I must close this entry now. My privacy is about to be interrupted by my wife.'

– – –

Irma had, as usual, made her presence felt long before her arrival. She was not a dainty walker, and her footsteps almost made the old house shudder as they thudded through it. She opened the door rather timidly, holding onto the handle.

'Uh, I'm not disturbing anything, am I? Uh. How's the book going?'

'Coming along, dear. Coming along. Just finished for today as a matter of fact. I was about to come and join you.'

'Oh, great, anyway. Anyway,' she started again, twisting the brass doorknob this way and that.

'Sit down, dear. You look tired.'

Her hair and face had been neglected during the past few days.

'Oh, yes, thanks. Anyway, I wanted to talk to you.'

'Go ahead.'

'You're not going to like this one little bit.'

'Oh?'

'No, and er what's more, it's kinda hard to say. So er just sit tight.'

'OK, I'm sitting tight.'

'Well it's about poor Ernest. I feel kinda sorry about the whole thing.'

'Don't we all, a most tragic occurrence, but I don't see...' Quakke was deliberately holding fire.

'No well you wouldn't. The fact is, well, Hymie darling, I'm going to come right out and say it. Ernest and I at that party of Lucy's, we went to bed together. I don't mean actually bed, because it was in the garden and rather damp, and not at all comfortable like bed, but, well, you see, don't you?'

'I see,' said Quakke, which was nothing less than the truth.

'Well, and then poor Ernest, he was so happy too when he went home, and then going and killing himself like that. Oh Hymie, it's so horrible. You don't know what I've been through these past few days.' She flung herself at him with a resounding thump so that he nearly fell off his chair, but just managed to maintain them both at the minimum point of equilibrium and to pat her on the back and comfort her. It was an unusual role for him in the household and one which despite the circumstances, he couldn't help enjoying.

'The Coroner said nothing about suicide, Irma,' Quakke said quietly.. 'He said it was an accident.'

'Yes, but I know better,' sobbed Irma. 'That poor man, eaten with agony and remorse and...'

'There, there.' Quakke was warming to his role.

'And I only wanted to comfort him because his wife wasn't there and to look after him, you know.'

'That was always your trouble.'

Irma did not hear.

'Things just got out of hand. It was a party after all.'

Hymer tried hard to see the logic of this. Was it in the nature of things for parties to get out of hand or for people to get out of hand at parties? Or did it depend on the people? He couldn't remember anything getting out of hand.

'I mean he took me by surprise, not at all the kind of thing one expects from a clergyman. I mean, don't think I'd go down the garden with anybody, honey. I felt kinda sorry for him. Perhaps his wife didn't understand him or something. He was a perfect gentleman, of course, but, oh Hymie, say you forgive me. I've suffered so much and even if you forgive me I shall only be quits with you and not with poor Letitia, and I shall never forgive myself, never.' She burst into tears again. Quakke felt his shirt beginning to get wet. It was almost as though his organs were misplaced and he had wet himself. It was warm and unpleasant and the role of comforter began to feel more burdensome.

He ignored her pleas, simply patted her on the back repeatedly.

'What you appear to be saying in a rather confused way, so much so that you yourself have not realised its significance, is that the initiative came from Mann, even though you were, so to speak, receptive to his advances. A mature man must after all take responsibility for himself and decide how he shall act.'

'Oh it sounds so callous, Hymie. Perhaps you're right. Still, if I hadn't been there and all and maybe encouraged him, he'd still be here now wouldn't he?'

'If, my dear, if. What a strange word to apply to the past. An unreal condition. At least we can put another 'if' against it. If he hadn't died that way, who knows that he might not have died in another, perhaps a more gruesome, way? Whatever you may say, his time had come, whether you had a part large or small in the business or not. Now stop upsetting yourself. You're not to blame. Come on, we'll both go and have a drink.'

He gave her an affectionate peck. He was enjoying himself again.

Irma was not entirely convinced but was certainly relieved and it suddenly occurred to her. Why was Hymer talking so much sense?

And 'ifs' began to come into her mind again. If Hymie had been there, there would have been no question of... If Hymie wasn't there, where was he? Now that was an 'if' worth remembering.

'Have a drink, darling.'

Yes, there was something different.

– – –

'No thank you, not today,' said Lucy in her briskest housewife-like tones to the red-blonde haired youth standing at her door. 'I don't know what you're selling, but I'm sure I have quite enough of it already. Good day.'

She made to slam the door, but an intruding boot held it ajar, and a wide grin registered victory.

'Look lady,' said Logos tolerantly. Kronos always said public relations was not his line but he had a kind of affection for his unique combination of naivete and wickedness. 'I ain't selling nothing.'

'Then kindly tell me what business you have disturbing me and then go away,' Lucy's lips pursed angrily.

'Well nah. Vat does look beautiful when you pout like vat. Supposing I were to say you might do something for me.' He grinned again. Lucy was beginning to like him as she very quickly did all men. After all it was a couple of hours before Titus came home and there wasn't much danger from men, she thought, if you let them have what most of them wanted.

'Come in.'

'Nah that's more reasonable, most reasonable if I might say so, Mrs Lastick, or shall I call you Lucy?'

'How do you know my name?' Perhaps this was something really sinister after all.

'We 'as our mefods, we 'as our mefods,' replied Logos, looking round the drawing room he had just been shown into.

'Nice place you got here,' he said predictably, ignoring Lucy's further efforts to get out of him what he was really there for.

'Well at least tell me your name,' she said in exasperation.

'Tell you what,' he winked. 'How's about having a little guessing game? You tell me what my name is and every time you get it wrong, I give you a little kiss, just for compensation you understand.'

Lucy felt more at ease. This was more up her street. Perhaps Kronos was wrong. At least Logos' public relations appeared to be getting results.

They both sat down on the settee and Logos put his arm around Lucy, who giggled as though it were the first time. In a sense, it was.

'Here's a kiss just to start you off. There now, away you go. Guess away to your heart's content.'

'Thompson'

'No' (kiss)

'Wilson'

'No' (kiss)

'Bastaple'

'No' (kiss) etc.

'Oh, come on,' said Lucy after a score or more tries, not worried to be losing, but slightly pained as she always was not to be winning.

'Would you believe Smiff?'

'No,' said Lucy.

'Alright then, it's Jones. Vat's it Olwen Jones, Welsh you see on my farver's side.'

'Silly,' coughed Lucy. 'Olwen's a girl's name. you aren't a girl, are you?'

'Dunno. I suppose we could find out though. Come here you lovely bit of...' He pushed her onto her back, a position not entirely new to her, and began to make extravagant imitations of rape.

'Get off,' said Lucy, helpless with laughter.

'Right then. Tell you what.' The grin spread right up to his ear. 'Bit more sport. Bit more sport. You guess how old I am and just for a bit of variety, you take off one item of clothing every time you guess wrong.'

'Oh,' said Lucy, surprised at his impertinence. 'I'm not wearing much.' She giggled again.

'Yeah, well, won't take long, will it? One shoe counts as one by the way. Start wiv the little uns like earrings. More exciting like innit? Ready, steady, go.'

'Eighteen'

'Nah'

Lucy took off an earring, placing it carefully on the coffee table.

'Oho, sexy,' taunted Logos.

'Nineteen'

'Nah'

One more earring.

'Cor, the revelation is stupendous. You should never wear earrings. You'd drive all the men wild you would.'

'I'm beginning to wish I had half a dozen ears,' joked Lucy.

'Come off it.'

'Twenty four'

One shoe.

'More or less?'

'Ah that'd be telling'

'Twenty one'

'Nope'

Two shoes.

'Twenty six'

'Nope. Jumper nah dahling.'

The desired garment removed.

'Twenty two'

'Nah, skint. Here I'll give you a hand. Two in fact. Huhoo.'

'I'm starting to forget now. Twenty.'

'Not on your life. Bra. Cor you aren't bad, are you? Two hands for vat.'

'Twenty three'

'No. Tights.'

Lucy wriggled out of them. 'You're cheating,' she accused.

'Yep,' said Logos phlegmatically. 'No point in losing. Take your knickers off, ven I'll have a go at guessing how much you weigh to the nearest pound. Same rules. An I fink I'll have half a stone's worth straight off.' He licked his lips as Lucy literally climbed out of her last piece of apparel and put her arms round him.

– – –

'Vat warn't bad,' exclaimed Logos when Lucy was dressing again. 'I bet you've done vat a few times before haven't you? Come on nah own up. And wiv a few more than your husband eh?' The grim mechanism began to work again as though it were worked by a skilful ventriloquist. 'I'll tell you somefing. Vat's one of the best I've ever had dahling.' He was not one to be loath to damn with faint praise.

Lucy looked a trifle hurt.

'Ah come on nah dahling, don't you take any notice of old women like Olwen.'

He had found a formula again. She smiled, though not, it is true, as devastatingly as Logos.

'I hear you have, like, a lot of parties here. Good are they?'

'Of course.'

'Plenty of fun, know what I mean? Bit of the old how's yer farver?'

'Well yes, if you put it like that, it does happen.' Now she had been served by this young animal, the hostess was beginning to be revolted by his coarseness.

'Heard about some of the goings-on. Randy parsons 'aving it off wiv American girls while hostesses look after their husbands.'

Lucy coloured.

'Look here, I don't know how you know about all this but if blackmail's your line you've come to the wrong place. That's one game I most certainly do not play. My husband is well aware that, well, I have certain inclinations.'

'Ha ha. Vat's good. "Certain inclinations", I must remember that. Steady on, I ain't no blackmailer, more a sort of a social worker if you get my meaning, getting people together, yeah vat's it, getting people together.'

'I'm afraid I don't see...'

'You will, you will.'

'If this is another of your jokes...'

'You've had enough for one day. I know love, I know.' He caressed her knee affectionately.

'Just a friendly word of warning. These American dames don't take too kindly to having their husbands pinched, part of the wild west training y'see. Ain't averse to coming gunning for you some of 'em. Not to say that this Quakke woman ain't probably a peace-loving little gel, soft-hearted like and might let you off with a warning. If she got to know of course. Not saying she will, but I should be on my guard if I was you. Be prepared for anything so to speak. She might never know of course.'

'Look, I could let you have a few thousand...'

'Never touch the stuff. Sorry dahling. Well, better be going nah. Fanks for the parlour games anyway. Toodle pip.'

'Wait,' cried Lucy. 'Who are you?'

But he was gone. He hadn't even waited to notice she was trembling.

She remained motionless there on the settee for a while not thinking of anything. The whole business was a stupefying shock. She had never been confronted before with complications to her amorous frolics, probably because that's all they were. There was little danger to family security from any of them, adulterous or no. Affairs, she used to tell herself, caused tragedies. A 'romp in the hay' was comedy itself. If there was the remotest chance of the romp developing into an affair she stopped it immediately.

She took a long cigarette from the silver box near her right hand, used the table lighter more extravagantly than necessary on it and blew out long streaks of smoke from tightly pursed lips.

What had Smith or Jones or whatever his name was actually said and how did he know anyway? It was like some kind of ghostly supernatural intervention. She shuddered. Never mind that she told herself. What had he said? Something about "goings-on". Randy parsons – revolting language – 'aving it off with American girls and hostesses looking after their husbands. She had thought more about the second charge than the first, it directly concerning her. Well it was a nice little romp and Lucy had enjoyed it more than most. He looked as though he'd never touched a woman for years. But what about randy parsons? So that was what Irma Quakke had been so silent for? So that's what went on? Well she would have something to say to Mrs Quakke even if she were as possessive as the erstwhile visitor seemed to suggest. Would she have time though? Wild west traditions, he had said. Shoot first, ask questions afterwards.

She dropped her cigarette which was burning her fingers, then deftly nipped it from the floor and put it into an ash tray.

Perhaps, as he had said, it would be better to be prepared for anything.

– – –

The next morning Quakke got a letter. He read it at the breakfast table with badly concealed surprise.

'Anything interesting, dear?' spluttered Irma through a mouthful of toast.

'No, no,' said Hymer. 'Just a bill, that's all.'

'No bills due as far as I can see, Hymie.' The toast took another unexpected assault.

'It's nothing. I've told you.'

'Now come on, Hymie. That's not like you. Let me see.'

She was out of her chair and had snatched the letter from the table before he knew what was happening. And she had been asking herself the same question time and time again. 'If Hymie wasn't there, where was he?'

She got the answer suddenly, and in a way she had not expected. As she fell back into her seat she knocked over her coffee cup and spilt the hot liquid all over her knees but she paid no attention to it. She unfolded the paper.

It was typed and said quite simply, 'Who was that lady you were with on Saturday night?'

'Well,' said Irma sharply, 'who was it? How could you do this to me, Hymie, your poor dear Irma? I thought something strange was going on. You haven't been yourself at all. Hymie, who was it for heaven's sake? Don't keep me in suspense any longer. Who is this woman who stole my husband?' In the heat of the moment she had forgotten her own troubles.

'Would it make any difference if you knew? After all, it does take two.'

'You mean it was your fault? Oh, come off it, Hymie, you know what an angel you are, or were. Why, Hymer Quakke, how could you betray your Irma like this? And where? I couldn't have been more than forty paces away all the time.'

'Perhaps you were down the garden path,' said Hymer thoughtfully.

'Oh no,' sighed Irma who took his point. 'What a mess, Hymie, what a mess. Still, I won't let you get away with it just like that. You're going to tell me who it was.'

'Don't you think it would be better for us to go to the police first?'

'What in heaven's name for?'

'Anonymous letter. The police are interested in that sort of thing.'

'You're trying to distract me again, Hymie. Anonymous letter it may be, nasty, cheap, underhand thing it may be, but I don't see any threat in it, and I somehow don't think there'll be any more, do you, Hymie?'

'No.' It was true he felt no shame or guilt but he felt very uncomfortable for all that. He took a strong gulp of coffee and coughed because it burned his throat.

'There you see, guilt. That's what it is. Now don't tell me I'll guess. It was that Lastick woman, wasn't it? I've seen her type before. Well she's dropped her pants in the wrong direction this time. I saw her looking at you. I wondered why she seemed so interested in you. That's it, isn't it, Lucy Lastick?'

Quakke nodded. He was about ready to tell her why, but she never asked. She merely sat down in her place and wept. It was the sort of scene Nathalie Weinburger went to see at the drive-in every week and which she loved either in fiction or in fact. Quakke thought ruefully that she would enjoy seeing it even among her friends.

'I'm going into London now,' said Hymer. 'I shan't be back for lunch.

Irma made no attempt to stop him. She had not needed to tell him where she was going. He had known he could not prevent her and so had withdrawn without wasted effort from the arena.

– – –

'I didn't hear you come in last night.'

'Nah, well, didn't want to disturb anybody.' Logos bit sadistically on an apple.

'How did it go?'

'Well, you know me, Kronos, full of charm and enticement for the opposite sex.'

'I do know you. That's why I asked.'

'Worked like a charm. Got the old pussy really frightened I did. 'Ere ain't bad is she?'

'I do not like to hear my friends referred to as "old pussies", Logos. I think someone like her rates a little higher than "not bad". An exceedingly accomplished woman, I should say. I hope you weren't too brutal with her.'

'Nah. Gentle as a kitten. You know me.'

'Precisely.'

'We 'ad a few diverting games, vat's all.'

'I hope so for your sake.'

'If you're so worked up about her, why send me?'

'Because you must learn sometime the way to handle people, the best people.'

He hesitated.

'Learning, however, is a harsh process. It involves at every stage a complete awareness of one's duty to oneself and to other people. The freedom I gave you carries with it heavy responsibility. I hope you are aware of that my friend. Because if you have failed, you and no one else will suffer for it. Do we understand each other?'

'Yeh, I fink so.'

'Good grief. Do you learn nothing? Thinking, what is that? That is merely the beginning of a process. To act correctly we must be convinced.'

'Alright then, I'm convinced.'

'Good. We shall wait and see the results of your operation.'

'It'll be all right, Kronos. I said so.'

'Very well.'

– – –

After Hymer had gone, Irma didn't waste very much time. She went upstairs, dressed quickly, casting the occasional glance at the mirror to see what it was that didn't satisfy her husband any more, shrugged her shoulders on being unable to find anything, dashed downstairs again, pulled her Cadillac laboriously out of the ditch where she had parked it the previous evening, and making various inspections in the driving mirror, drove as fast as was legally impossible to Lucy's.

'Rotten bitch,' she kept muttering to herself, 'dirty rotten bitch. Well, I'll tell her a thing or two.'

– – –

It would be untrue to say she was welcomed at the door by Lucy. Nevertheless she was admitted without much ceremony and found herself seated in the very same place occupied not so long ago by Logos in spite of her loud protests that what she had to say would not take long and it wasn't worth sitting down. She took a drink, a gin and tonic, again in spite of herself.

Possibly because she feared she was being coaxed into calmness, pacified by little insignificant acts of hospitality, she began more brutally and clumsily than she had intended.

'Now look here,' she took a good long swallow to calm her palpitations, ' you know why I've come to see you so let's not beat around the bush.'

'I'm sorry Irma dear, but I don't see...' She was outwardly very offhand, but had visions of a wild stallion being let out of its gate, a stallion she had to ride on pain of being trampled under its prancing hooves. She felt the dust and the awful animal stench, the sweat beginning to pour from her brow.

'You see alright. You see a damned sight too well. Your eyes are keen enough when it comes to sizing up what other women's men have inside their pants, well this time you've bitten off more than you can chew.' The figure of speech would have been amusingly inappropriate in other circumstances, but nobody noticed it.

'You dirty rotten bitch,' Irma began again, taking another gulp of gin. 'You daughter of a whore, you strumpet, you wife-stealing tart.' She was becoming confused. This gave Lucy the chance she wanted to pull herself together, to be sarcastic, to turn the broadsword with the rapier.

'At least my dear...' she said slowly but still trembling from her opponent's onslaught.

'Don't you call me my dear. Save that for your whoremongers, your fancy men, and keep your thieving hips off decent men.'

'At least my dear,' repeated Lucy, not to be put off, 'I am in the right company, as I'm sure our mutual friend Letitia Mann would agree if she were aware of, shall we say, certain indiscretions which went on at that jolly party of mine.'

'What do you mean?' gabbled Irma, fencing. It had incredibly never occurred to her that the same people who knew about Hymer and Lucy were unlikely to have been unaware of her and Mann, but she did see now what a good job whoever it was had made of it.

'Who told you?' she said after a moment.

'I wish I could tell you my dear, but I am as much in the dark about that as you are.'

'Whoever it was made a damned good job of the whole business. we had a practically untraceable anonymous letter this morning.'

'I see,' said Lucy, 'but you must agree that well, under the circumstances, your action had far more tragic consequences than mine. I mean, poor Ernest, and poor Letitia.'

'Well I grant you my mind hasn't been exactly easy these past few days, but how do you think I feel having my husband seduced under my very nose. It's almost as bad as having him bumped off.'

'But my dear,' smiled Lucy. Her pretence of calmness was enough to irritate Irma.

'As I saw it, it was rather the other way round. I admit that the prospect of a new conquest was not far from my mind, but when it came down to it, I was the one who was conquered.'

'You're lying. That dear boy has never looked at another woman in the whole of his married life and then some cheap tart hiding under the guise of her husband's position and respectability goes and floors him in one fell swoop.'

The last taunt was too much for Lucy. She could have stood most things but she could not bear being called "cheap".

"Well, let me tell you something now. You've had your say, now let me have mine. Your husband took me, not cheaply, no, because for a few minutes he could be himself with me, because we could take each other as we were and give ourselves, because he didn't have to worry about pretending to be excited by your overweening, overbearing, cheap, yes cheap, artificial tendencies. I may have my faults, Mrs Quakke, but I think about other people. I give myself to them completely. I don't do it in the first place for my pleasure but for theirs. You get your kicks out of doing a favour for Hymie, you great condescending Lady Bountiful. Well that's something I can't stand.'

'It's not true,' flushed Irma.

She got hold of Lucy's hair with a force which looked sure to pull it right out of its roots and shook her violently like a rag doll till her eyes almost popped out of their sockets.

Lucy literally tore herself away and just as Irma was about to renew the onslaught ran a long steel paper-knife through her stomach.

As she put up her hands to her face in horror she felt them sticky with blood. It was so realistic she thought it must be fictitious. She dropped over Irma whispering words of comfort and encouragement but Irma merely groaned and groaned.

When she recovered herself sufficiently to call the police Irma had already lost a lot of blood.

Lucy replaced the receiver, stood for a moment contemplating the results of her handiwork, then sank stunned to the settee.

– – –

Ten minutes later the natives of Tolbridge were surprised to see entering the drive of the Lastick residence an ambulance, followed closely by a police car.

'I thought there'd be trouble there one of these fine days,' said a local Solomon, one of those all too common wise men after the event.

Quakke was still in London where no one knew he had gone. Lastick rushed home from the factory where he had at first been angry when his board meeting was interrupted. These facts are recorded merely because they happened. There is perhaps nothing particularly significant or interesting in either of them.

Perhaps it should also be mentioned that the inspector who called to see Lucy was a red-haired man with a moustache like a carrot which he kept biting as though to stimulate thought. He also had a wart under his left ear which was thought by some to have hindered his promotion to Chief Inspector. Perhaps it indicated to the observant a lack of ruthlessness.

His assistant, however, a handsome young man with a good physique, was said to be so like a television policeman that he would be bound to get on.

Part Two

– – –

Chapter One

'I should have stopped her,' mused Quakke. 'Yes, I should have darned well stopped her, promised to leave the district or something. Anything to avoid these damnable scenes.'

He bit his lip remorsefully. He began to wish he had not given up smoking. So much for self-improvement. He had just approached Trafalgar Square and he sat down on a bench, carefully spreading a newspaper to protect himself from damp and pigeon-droppings. He had already spent the night in a dank and dingy little flat which he had rented for two weeks to think things out. The walls were coated with a veneer of stale fat, which, combined with his improved sense of smell since he had renounced the weed, was beginning to put him off his favourite food.

'I'll call her: she'll have calmed down by now. I don't have to tell her where I am.'

Having made the resolution, he got up, and picking up the newspaper he had not even bothered to read in his previous turmoil, he was transfixed with horror at the headline:

"DEATH STRIKES AGAIN IN SLEEPY VILLAGE"

He did not have to read much further to know that he would not be speaking to Irma again, except perhaps in the company of the blessed angels. He sloped off reluctantly to do his duty.

– – –

The trial was straightforward. There was not much Lucy was able to deny. She was convicted of murder by a judge who refused to admit of any mitigating circumstances. Violence might have been understandable in a man, but if one started tolerating it in a woman, there was no knowing what collapse in private morals might ensue. Lucy was sent down for that portion of life which would be practical and attenuated by good behaviour.

Quakke, who had never believed for a moment that there was anything but exuberant innocence in Lucy, had thought it prudent, nevertheless to spend an extended period of mourning after the funeral rites. But suspicions that he had had some influence over Lucy, which, as we have seen, had not helped Lucy's case, were not allayed by this tactic and the discovery that Lucy was pregnant by him gave one of those meals to the tabloid press that they are only too anxious to wolf down.

Quakke now found himself facing the prospect of fatherhood for the first time in his life, and, since Lastick had been persuaded by his many business "friends" that it was advisable to start divorce proceedings against Lucy, the opportunity of marrying for a second time.

'You don't have to, you know,' she had said to him.

'I know,' he had replied with his new found composure, 'that's the attraction of it.' And Lucy had burst into tears because for her also it was a liberation.

– – –

Quakke had been trying hard to understand the sudden upheaval which had taken place in Tolbridge. At this stage he wrote in his diary:

'It may be that there are forces of evil older than our present society and rooted in the mind of man himself – I speak generically of course. What Society permits may never have as great or disastrous effect as what it cannot control.'

In other words, the circumstances which had led to the deaths of Mann and Irma were not just the outcome of promiscuous behaviour. Guilt – there was an evil, certainly if over-experienced – witness poor Ernest – whilst Quakke was sure that Lastick had been up to something he could easily accommodate with his ten-bedroom conscience. He had had plenty of practice at it. Jealousy – that had been the undoing of Irma, jealousy which had blinded her to her own shortcomings. She had acted in character, but out of convention. Then there had been the typed note. At her trial, Lucy had denied sending it. Nobody had been able to establish who had sent it, and after all, the police weren't interested. They had their self-confessed culprit. The whole thing was cut and dried.

It suddenly became clear to Hymer who had had his mind occupied with so many other matters over the past few months, that if he found the sender of the note he would get to the bottom of the Tolbridge affair. This may seem obvious to the reader, but for Quakke it was a total revolution in his way of thinking. He was more used to inventing answers and then making up the questions to fit them. This habit, I am sure, did not extend to others in his profession, where meticulous collection and interpretation of evidence were vital tools. Quakke had never done detective work before.

Time for some suspects then. He could vaguely remember who had been at the fateful party, although it was the first time he had met some of them. It couldn't have been Lastick himself. He was used to Lucy's goings-on and any way, if he'd been annoyed, he was quite big enough to look after himself, not send notes implicating other people. The film producer...we...ll possibly, but – wait a minute! – what about those oddballs who turned up late? Could one of them have been snooping? He would get Lucy to remind him of who they were. Then he remembered the demo. One of them had organised the demo. What was his name now? How near Quakke actually was to the truth he was unaware, but if he had been, what could he prove?

– – –

Lucy quickly identified her longish acquaintance with Julian.

'He's been so helpful to me over this whole thing, the darling. I can't tell you what I'd have done without him, especially with you not being here and all that.'

'Oh well, I suppose that leaves him out,' thought Quakke.

'I don't know much about the other two, though. Don't know where the girl got to on the night of the party, as a matter of fact. Same place as us, I expect. I got rid of the blonde one as soon as I could. I was only after you that night, remember?'

Quakke could.

'Anyway,' continued Lucy, 'What does it matter now? I've got my sentence to do and that's that.'

'We could appeal.'

'On what grounds? New evidence? There isn't any.'

'There's something odd going on, Lucy. I know Ernest is supposed to have killed himself and you killed Irma, but it wasn't your fault, don't you see?'

'No, not really.' Lovely girl that she was, Lucy had never been a runner in the brain stakes.

'Is there anybody who could have known about you and me and sent that note?'

'No..oo,' Lucy seemed to be convincing herself.

'Sure?'

'Sure, except...' she hesitated.

'Go on.'

'Except the red-haired guy who called round and played some games.'

'Played some games! What does that mean for Christ's sake?' Blasphemy had not yet come onto Hymer's schedule of improvement.

'Well, you know.'

'I think I do by now,' said Quakke, sighing heavily. 'Who the hell was he?'

'Said his name was Smith or Jones or something. He was just trying to blackmail me, I thought, but when I offered him money he wouldn't take it.'

'Just trying to... Lucy, you are the absolute... and you'd never seen him before? He wasn't at the party?'

'No, that's what I can't understand, unless... His voice was vaguely familiar.'

'Could he have been one of the three stooges?'

'He had red hair.'

'People have been known to change more than their briefs, Lucy!'

Hymer Quakke had quickly learnt some things he was anxious to know and others he would rather not have known at all. He was convinced that the red-haired man had something to do with the deaths of Ernest and Irma. He asked Lucy to find out from her handsome friend, quite innocently of course, how his two companions were getting on. On Friday he had confided to his diary:

'Someone once said that for evil to flourish it was enough for good men to remain silent. These people must be caught. I do not know where or who they are. Least of all do I know why they should have caused the deaths of two innocent souls, but I shall not rest until they are found and punished.'

Chapter Two

Unknown to Quakke, an arrest had already been made. An early-morning call at the basement flat in Bullugly Road had found our well known trio lying haphazardly among the debris of a celebration – Champagne bottles, half-smoked cigarettes and cigars, scraps of food, glasses, articles of a more delicate nature.

– – –

'We've been interested in your activities for some time.' The tall, erect, pin-striped, good-mannered man reached for a decanter and poured himself and the dark man generous qualities of single malt.

'Whilst there are some nuances of ineptitude in your operation, we think you may be useful to us,' he continued.

'We are a free organisation...' began the dark man.

'Free? Mr.. er.. Kronos,' smiled the other, teasingly. 'None of us is free, my dear boy. If I may say so, you already show signs of enslaving yourself to the nefarious activities of your little clique. Those last two pieces of er... recreational euthanasia were a little close together. Your male friend, in particular, needs careful handling. Still we are good at that. But I digress too much at this stage. Where was I? Ah yes freedom. It is a common saying that this is a free country, but it isn't of course. We all have our several duties... our very several duties. Mine is to see that this great country of ours is preserved intact from social upheaval, that its traditions are upheld, that it is properly governed irrespective of whom is elected to its offices of state or indeed who sits on its throne. There are some developments in our present society which allow people to think they are liberated. Sexual tolerances, comprehensive schools, you know the sort of thing, I'm quite sure. We welcome these. We are not concerned at the pursuit of individualism. Indeed that is just what we want to encourage. Selfless, collective activity is our enemy. You have shown that you can use this kind of activity for your own ends. You are now going to help us subvert systematically public shows of solidarity whenever they occur.

'Law and order, you mean,' said Kronos, sipping thoughtfully.

'Order, certainly,' the pin-stripe nodded approvingly. 'Control, but I'm glad you mentioned Law, because we are quite prepared to use it, to invest in its moral blackmail – a nasty word, I'm sorry – and of course, in your case...'

'I see,' sighed Kronos, 'if we refuse to co-operate, some convenient charge might easily be levelled against us.'

'Precisely.' Pin-stripe grinned with satisfaction. 'We know the sorts of things you've been up to.' He threw onto the leather desk-top a heavy file. 'Conspiracy to murder, actual murder, that sort of thing. I knew you were an intelligent man, Mr Kronos.'

'So, what do we have to do?'

'Lie low for a bit. Just wait for our instructions. Keep out of the way. We've arranged a little holiday for you in Scotland – at our expense, of course. Do have a good time. Goodbye, Mr Kronos. We shall not meet again. Just do as you are instructed and, believe me, you will be well rewarded.

'Cock it up, and we shall land on you like a ton of bricks,' grumbled Kronos. For the first time he understood the meaning of "an offer you can't refuse".

'Precisely, although not too happily expressed,' smiled Pin-stripe. 'By the way – I probably don't need to tell you – this conversation has never taken place. Goodbye.'

'Mamma is the word,' Kronos gulped down his whisky and left the room.

– – –

Over a number of years the members of ARE and many others, who by their criminal tendencies had rendered themselves eminently suitable to serve the nation, did indeed prosper. Fear was growing apace in the minds of the public that, whilst they enjoyed tremendous freedom individually, the rights and freedom of groups were a great danger to them, that they needed strong government to look after them. This was not the first time such a tactic had been employed, nor indeed would it be the last.

There was barely a demonstration by whatever action group went by, but that it was made clear by the media that there were dangerous attempts being made on democracy which must be resisted at all costs. This was ironically true. Kronos and his ilk saw to all the details which would look good on the evening news broadcasts. They would start trouble between the police and demonstrators, light the navy blue touch-paper, in other words, then retire. With their background, ARE found it easy money. Sometimes they would escape arrest altogether with all the threat that that implied for future demonstrations. More often they would be among others arrested and released without charge.

'What was the world coming to?' the man in the street, or more likely hiding behind closed doors, would be asking himself. He could not even go to a football match without fear of violence. The products of the permissive society were only too clear. In this theatre of action Logos came into his element, organising hit gangs who travelled from city to city causing mayhem on the terraces and giving reputations to well known football clubs they would rather have done without.

Kaki became a prominent feminist, playing her role in emasculating the male population with demands for orgasms a la carte fror women and claiming full participation in all walks of life, right up to the highest political office in the land. At least this last claim was unlikely, men told themselves.

Yet all these things happened so naturally that only dangerous, irresponsible, anarchistic minorities could be blamed.

On occasions, even, opposition to the government of the day was encouraged. A 'one nation' government was perceived to have been brought down by the activities of miners and other trade unionists. However, there was no need to fear the enemy within. With friends like Pin-stripe the country did not need enemies.

Quakke had now totally abandoned his writing – apart from his diary, that is – although it had been incomprehensible enough to gain him a lectureship at a provincial university where he had eventually risen to the Chair of Methodology. He didn't believe in any of that rubbish any more, but he was quite happy in a 1984 which had not, some said, turned out to be anything quite so bad as Orwell's predictions, to be peddling the new version of double-duckspeak. In the right persuasion mode, he had easily convinced himself that flexibility was the 4th dimension of good planning and, since he had a wife and teenage daughter to support, to plan to have a steady income was a sound strategic procedure.

He had not totally abandoned the idea of locating the perpetrator of events in Tolbridge, but he had drawn a complete blank. Evidence and people seemed to have mysteriously disappeared. The typewritten note which was of so little consequence, it appeared, to either defence or prosecution, and had easily been obtained on request by Quakke, had been 'mislaid' in a minor burglary in the Professor's former abode in which a few trinkets, several meerschaum pipes and a portable television had been taken. These were obviously, according to the police, adequate motives for the break-in and attempts by Hymer to impute pretexts more sinister were met with a stony silence. As for characters we have previously encountered and whose purposes are known to us, if not to Quakke, their transformation had been such that they had been put – for the time being at any rate – beyond suspicion.

Sir Julian Callendar, now a pin-stripe-toting top civil servant had visited Lucy when she was in prison, had been very kind to her and had secured privileges for her for which even Quakke in his new self-sufficiency had been grateful. Attempts by our hero to gain knowledge of what the trio had been up to at the demo, at the party and, in the case of the young blonde man who was now dismissed as 'a mere casual acquaintance, dear boy,' after the party, were shrugged off by Callendar with an ease which was now second nature to him. However, Quakke was not convinced that 'raking up the past would do nobody any good'.

Fritzy Freeman, the rather rough diamond – if diamond at all – was a successful businessman and Chairman of the First Division football club, Chesterham United. The supporters loved him. He behaved as though he understood them, and indeed he had, as we have seen, spent some time with the rougher elements. His special mission now, however, was to clean up the image of the game, and this, apart from the odd crowd or travel disturbance he organised at home and abroad, just to keep people nice and anxious and look to the authorities for protection, he did to the best of his ability. In this work of national importance he came under the overall control of Sir Julian Callendar, Head of Special Targets Office, which, of course, as far as the general public, the Government, the Armed Forces and the Civil Service were concerned, did not exist.

As for the lovely Julie. Who could have better credentials than a half-caste, feminist lesbian who was constantly in the eye of the public, who oozed political correctness from every pore, and moreover, was admired by Lucy and her equally lovely daughter Gemma?

The best place to hide a pebble is, undoubtedly, on the beach.

— — —

The Tolbridge affair, therefore, without being entirely wiped from memory, had receded into the back of a mind more occupied with academic success and blissful domestic arrangements. It had been a struggle bringing up Gemma while Lucy had remained in prison, but Quakke felt he had made a pretty good job of it. His wife thought so too and when she eventually emerged from the gloom of incarceration was privileged, she felt, to enjoy for just a few years those teenage times when the relationship between mother and daughter seems make or break. Gemma had grown into a beautiful, confident and well-balanced young woman. At eighteen she had won a place to read Politics at Oxford and was making the most of the now customary year out before taking it up. Partly, it must be admitted, her father's status, her own intelligence and a pound or two of pestering saw her engaged as a junior reporter on a provincial newspaper in the little Yorkshire town of Grimeford. As miners gained a high profile in their fight to preserve jobs, she was increasingly finding commissions from national press agencies to report on trends and attitudes in the coalfields. Some resentment was inevitably felt by her Editor and more experienced colleagues, but Gemma was confident enough she could handle this, she told her father.

In many discussions, she and Quakke had agreed on the destructive potential and, indeed, actuality, of market forces in the increase in crime rates, the obsession with private gain, the obliteration of moral values, threats of privatisation of public utilities under the guise of efficiency, the 'trickle down' myth, the pretence that restrictions on services or benefits given to the less well-off were, actually, opportunities to savour.

Quakke wrote in his diary one Sunday, in what might be seen as a lay sermon:

'If so-called permissive trends have brought about anything at all, it is not the freedom of a majority of individuals, but enslavement to the great Market. A million or so women have been 'freed' from ties at home to take on low-paid, low-skilled jobs whilst traditional male occupations have declined. The gap between rich and poor is widening and local communities such as Gemma and I have discussed are bound for destruction. Male unemployment and the often concomitant single parenthood are contributing to this. Drugs, which are not permitted, but are increasingly seen as social anaesthesia among the disillusioned young, in particular, will cement social decline.'

Chapter Three

A meeting was being held of the committee of the Antidiluvian Club. Nothing unusual in that. It happened once a month on the third Sunday or on the fourth if there were five Sundays in the month. The usual business of a club was discussed as per the published Agenda. As in all clubs, however, it was the last item A.O.B. which provided the real interest for the assembled personages, who, it will be remarked, were a fairly exclusive bunch.

In addition to Sir Julian Callendar, Permanent Secretary to the Home Office, Sir James Weatherblown, Head of the Metropolitan Police, Field-Marshall Sir Hugh Carvem-Downe and Air Vice-Marshall Sir Duckham Hoyle there could be discerned a selection of millionaires, amongst whom Sir Fritzy Freeman, whose contributions, tax-deductible of course, were of vital importance in maintaining the Special Targets Office, to give its other name to the Committee of the Antidiluvian Club.

'I have to tell you,' harrumphed Sir Julian, knocking the ash from his half-smoked Havana and carefully adjusting the length of gold-linked cuff protruding from his jacket sleeve, that there will be a miners' strike this spring. They do not yet know this and I would be grateful if any among you have any miner friends, you would not mention it to them.' He paused for the laughter he expected to follow the joke, but with only a truncated guffaw emanating from Sir Duckham, he grunted and continued.

'I say they are unaware at the moment but, of course, over the past decade there has been a great deal of unrest in the coalfields. You'll remember all that dreadful business with Heath. Well, your Inner

Cabinet – he referred to himself, Fritzy and a well-known female broadcaster – has decided that this time they will strike and they will be beaten. Things will be messy. Maintaining an appearance of Democracy is a tricky business, but I think with the Government's and the media's help on the superficial features, we can just about maintain public animosity against the miners whilst minimising the disruption of the economy.'

Grunts of approval came from those who, above all, wished their economy to be undisrupted.

'There'll be no power cuts or 3-day weeks then?' asked George Ganz, a large machine-tool manufacturer from the Midlands who had a nice order building up from the Middle East with Government backing.

'No. Coal stocks will be high. We have already started moving it around to those places where it will be most needed. Just to rub it in, we shall import a few million tonnes of cheap slag from Poland or somewhere. This will have the added advantage that after the strike consumers will keep using it and close a few more pits down, but I don't deal with the details. Our field agents do that.'

'Once knew a cheap slag from Poland, meself,' muttered Sir Hugh, waking momentarily from a brandy-fuelled snooze.

'Ye..es, precisely,' re-commenced Callendar, unamused but not intolerant, eyeing Sir Hugh over his gold half-moon spectacles.

'The miners are fighting pit closures this time and may, therefore, be persuaded to ballot for and maintain a long strike. We can always rely on the Nottingham chappies to do a bit of black-legging though, especially if, as our information shows, the national leadership is trying to avoid a ballot. The media will highlight the illegality of this, of course. We've managed to get the Government to make some pretty natty anti-union laws recently in spite of the misgivings they were having about their popularity. We have plenty of agents in the press and on the airwaves who will soon put in the Law and Order boot, dish out the dirt when it comes to moving Union funds to Switzerland, accepting gifts from Commie-Republics, that sort of thing.'

'Will we get any direct action, like?'

'Certainly, Sir Fritz. I am sure if you want to involve yourself er... directly, but discreetly I must emphasize, er... something could be arranged. Did you have anything particular in mind?' Pin-stripe had been right. This man needed careful handling.

'Well, a few cavalry charges, beat 'em up, show 'em who's boss. Get some of them layabouts in the army to come and create a bit of aggro. We do kit 'em out and feed 'em for nuffin most of the time.'

'I say...' Sir Hugh had woken up again.

'Sorry, Hughie, no offence meant an' all that, but you must feel a bit like that yourself sometimes. You can't put 'em all up the Falklands or in Northern Ireland all the time. Get some o' them paratroopers kitted out as cops an' send 'em into the mining villages. Do that a few times an' you won't have no trouble for long.'

'Yes, well, we can always discuss details later,' sighed Sir Julian, 'but may I remind you of the necessity of making all this look perfectly natural and of making it last long enough for all the blame to be on the side of the miners and for the miners themselves never to want to do it again.'

'Well, then, we'll just rough 'em up a bit,' conceded Fritzy. Callendar knew the man was useful, but he had grown apart from him over the last fifteen years or so. There were times when he found his lack of couth tiresome, even nauseating. He made a mental note to get rid of Freeman once this business was over. After all the battle against democracy would be then to all intents and purposes won – for ever. Left-wing politics would be dead and buried.

'I take your point, anyway,' he continued. 'The very raison d'etre of the army is not, as those fools out there imagine, to defend them from some foreign johnnies. With what we spend on defence we couldn't do that in any case. Now and again we want a war with some tin-pot little banana republic to distract people's minds from what's going on here. But you're right. It is a proper use of the army to protect the integrity of this great country of ours from reds, pinks, or any colour of revolutionary, for that matter.'

Shouts of 'Hear! Hear!'

'That is, to maintain it as it is for the benefit of... er those who appreciate it.'

Shouts of 'Hear! Hear!'

'What about the Air Force then?' put in the Air Vice-Marshall who was wondering why he had turned up at all, except for the lunch, of course, which was always excellent on Antidiluvian Sundays.

'So nice of you to offer,' smiled Sir Julian, 'but we have to be a bit careful with the Air Force. It's our best advertising ploy, you know. Red Arrows, air sea rescue and so on. Now we can count on the media cooling things down for us from the police and army points of view, but they wouldn't like us using the Air Force.'

'Righty o, whizz on then, moral support it is.'

'I can concur absolutely with what Sir Julian has just been saying,' broke in a large, wheezy voice. It belonged to Lord Slack, proprietor of most of the nation's free press, Chairman of several television companies and part-time member of the Monopolies Commission. 'We can easily put the proper slant on things – show the right pictures, avoid showing the wrong pictures, dig up the dirt on the opposition, if things go wrong emphasize the unreliability of witnesses. And I do agree about the Air Force, Battle of Britain and all that. No, can't afford to risk tarnishing that sort of image. Lot of hard work went into building it up for a start.'

'Quite, quite,' muttered Sir Duckham. He was going to enjoy his lunch even more now that he had done his duty, but had been absolved from the consequences of it.

'Right, well, thank you all,' said Callendar with a satisfied smile, taking off his spectacles and rising from the Chairman's seat. 'Mr Secretary will, of course, record that, as there was no other business, the meeting concluded at 1-15 pm. Lunch, gentlemen?'

Chapter Four

Those readers who consider themselves expert in recognising the application of the sledgehammer to the nut may have been surprised at the strategies being discussed in our previous tableau. Pit closures there might have been and fifty or so others might be on an infamous 'hit list', but not all miners, it would appear, were equally concerned. Quakke, as we observed in his 'lay sermon', would no doubt have seen in this proof of his enslavement theory. Miners who were working and, moreover, earning good overtime money did not behave in a 'working class' mode any more, even though they still probably considered themselves as such. They had nice houses, large mortgages, wore fashionable clothes, enjoyed expensive holidays in exotic climes. Since January 1982 they had voted three times against strike action in national ballots, with the exception that is of certain areas which had suffered dramatic pit closures or who were traditionally or latterly more militant. They could well be expected to resist any calls for action from a leadership which was increasingly concerned about solidarity in its union, not only in opposition to pit closures, but also in respect to all redundancies. What the Antidiluvians were addressing was not a practical problem, as Sir Julian had pointed out, but a matter of principle, a matter of putting power squarely, if not fairly, back where it belonged.

In the Autumn of 1983 a new Chairman of the Coal Board thoughtfully gave the miners' leaders a twin pretext for industrial action. Coal was too expensive and collieries were producing too much of it. If their membership did not respond to calls to protect jobs alone, the leaders must have thought, the additional threat of continuing low pay increases would be bound to bring them on side. To start the ball rolling they called an overtime ban. The purpose of this seems unclear. If it was to reduce coal stocks and delivery to coal outlets then it was pointless. Gemma herself had described to her father the convoys of large vehicles of every kind she had seen moving in the early morning between pit and power station and between power station and power station to equalise stocks.

'Honestly, you wouldn't believe it, dad – furniture vans, grain lorries, anything that moves, practically. Gosh this is a bad line, isn't it? All that crackling, and the men only came to see it yesterday.'

At the time Quakke had thought she must be exaggerating, especially in the middle of a hot summer Sunday, but as he read his Autumn newspapers which claimed the overtime ban was having little or no effect as stocks were so high, he began to change his mind and determined to tell

Gemma next time he saw her personally to watch what she said over the telephone. A chill ran down his spine and for a moment he thought of the Tolbridge affair again.

If, on the other hand, the ban was intended to be a uniting tactic, there too it was unsuccessful. Some miners were losing a lot of money and some managements were able to minimise the effects of the ban by rescheduling shifts and meal-times. Right-wing candidates were pulling votes in local and national union elections.

Nevertheless, the fact that a majority of miners still supported the minimal show of strength represented by the overtime ban gave some encouragement to the leadership and, in the following Spring, when a large Yorkshire pit was closed without warning, legitimised by a previous ballot citing exactly this eventuality, a local strike began. This rapidly, and to the satisfaction of Special Targets Office, without a national ballot, soon spread to other areas.

– – –

'How's it going?' asked Sir Duckham as he gulped at a large whisky and soda in one of the far reaches of the Antidiluvian Club where totally confidential conversations were not only possible but positively encouraged

'Very well indeed,' smirked the tall dark man, his companion, flicking a speck of cigar ash from his pin-striped trousers and adjusting the creases as he sat down. 'We're in May now. Lovely weather. Perfect weather for a coal strike. Demand extremely low. Police don't really like riot control, but they're happy enough loafing around in this weather when things are quiet. Done a good job stopping flying pickets though. Been a bit over-zealous in one or two areas, by all accounts. Complaints coming in of chaps not being allowed out of pit villages to visit dying mothers and that sort of thing. Still, not to worry. Perhaps we ought to relax things a bit, let a few more through, have a bit of a showdown before public sympathy goes too far the other way. Things have swung a bit since that first week when we were fortunate to have that death on the picket line. I'll have a word with Fritzy, see what he can come up with. This could be just the thing to keep him quiet for a bit.'

'Yes, quite. Good show! Keep up the good work and all that.'

'We always aim to please,' said Callendar, reassuringly.

– – –

'Easy as pie an' mash,' said Fritzy, rubbing his hands gleefully when Sir Julian put the subject to him. 'Get some of the mounted up from the Met. They hate them Yorkshire bastards. You've no idea how much they look forward to Leeds United visits. We'll get our mob – SAS or somebody who ain't doing nuffin at the moment - to get a riot going, get out the way a bit smartish and then let the mounted lay into the tykes wiv their long batons.'

'Sounds good to me,' approved Sir Julian. 'I shall have a word with our friends in the media to see that we get the right coverage. By the way where will this take place?'

'There's a nice little coking plant near Sheffield, if I remember rightly – produces fuel for some steel works in Scunthorpe. By the way, do you know that joke about who put the cu...?'

'I do believe I have heard it a few hundred times,' sneered Callendar dismissively. 'What you have to do then is make sure you put the coke in Scunthorpe. We are going to make it appear that there will be very light policing around the plant, let as many pickets through as we can and keep the police reinforcements hidden round the corner. A nice little surprise, one might say.'

'Perfick,' smiled Fritzy. 'Absolutely perfick.'

– – –

Tim Glasby had only been a miner for eighteen months, but they had been the best eighteen months of his life. Bright enough at Grimeford Comprehensive School to be in the top band, he had, nonetheless, never taken to academic work, had excelled in the rugby team and left at sixteen and a half with two 'o' levels and three CSEs. His father, a miner like his father before him, seeing how things were going in the industry, had tried to persuade him earlier on to work hard at school, go to university maybe, escape from his dull surroundings, but at the age of fourteen or so had resigned himself to the fact that there would be one more generation of Glasbys down Grimeford Colliery. Tim had got on well with his early training and thought that later on he might train as a deputy or get some more qualifications and go into surveying or colliery management. For the moment he had been happy to have money in his pocket, to play rugby for the local club and with his rugged good looks – he was six foot three, with wiry blonde hair, and a fresh complexion – to pick up the girls on a Saturday night along with his best mates. Now he was on strike and he knew it was his future he was fighting for. He couldn't be bought off like the men in their late forties and fifties. He was in Arthur's army and proud of it.

As the plain transit van carrying himself and a dozen men from Grimeford moved out of the little town and onto the M18, he heard somebody up front say:

'No bloody rozzers today then: must be all waitin' for us dahn theer.'

'We were turned rahnd twice last week,' said somebody else.

'Bastards!' grunted another voice.

Tim was quiet. It was his first time.

'What's up wi' thee, then?' asked the lad next to him – Rob Bates, who had been at school with him since he was four and had never known him to be speechless for long. Usually they had got 'done' in lessons for talking together when boredom started to set in. 'Are tha brickin'?'

This reference to his bowels did not do much, in fact, to settle the enormous moths which seemed to be flying around inside Tim's stomach.

'Nah,' was his reply, said with bravado, but without conviction either for himself or his companions.

'Don't you worry, lad,' said an older man nearer the back of the van, 'we'll stuff them pigs just like we did at Saltley.'

'Aye we will an' all,' said the chorus of agreement.

'No fuckin' rozzer's gooin' ter ger 'owd o' me otherwise he'll get what's fuckin' comin' to 'im,' oathed another older and more experienced youth.

'That's what tha said last time, then when it came ter t'aggro tha ran sooa fuckin' fast ah thought thi arse were on fire,' put in a man in his early forties with a craggy pock-marked face.

'It wor. He were fuckin' crappin' 'issen,' shouted out Rob amid general laughter.

'Piss off,' snarled the object of their ridicule, unable to formulate a more crushing rejoinder.

'Ah bet Tim's thinking abaht yon lass, that fuckin' blonde reporter that were at t' pit gates yesterday. By eck, ah could fuckin' do summat fer her,' promised Billy Cooper, a thin, red-headed twenty-year old with burgeoning acne.

'Well, it'd make a change from doin' it to yer fuckin' self, yer wanker,' replied Tim.

'Tha's 'it a sore spot theer, Billy boy. Ah'd be careful wi' them posh bits if ah were thee, Tim,' said the forty-year old.

''Specially southerners, th'r' nowt but fuckin' cock-teasers. She's a bit too much class fer thee. Father's a professor, they tell me.'

'Aw, shut yer bleedin' gob,' said Rob, anxious now the chips were down to defend his mate.

'And are you gooin' ter mek me?' threatened the older man.

'Save it, lads, save it,' cut in Bill Jones, who was in charge of the picketing squad. He knew they had to let off steam. It helped them to settle down, but he also knew from long experience when to step in. 'We've a job to do here and we're going to do a good job. If I find any of youse have been drinking it'll be the last time you're trusted to do anything in this union. You're being paid to picket and picket you will. You will not show physical violence to anybody – if you have to defend yourself that's a different matter – and you can save your shouting and sneering for later. Them's the rules and as a Union Official I am officially telling you. Break them rules and you go on no more pickets. Understand?'

The grumbles of not too reluctant agreement subsided and the van progressed in relative peace and tranquillity towards its destination.

– – –

Gemma smiled as she thought of how her father had tried to persuade her to give up the journalism business. He was, apparently, concerned at the way things were developing in the coalfields and considered she would be better out of it. Like Tim's father, however, he had known when to give up and contented himself with pleas for her to be careful:

'You could get mixed up in something awfully complicated. There's a lot at stake here, you know. Remember all you told me about the preparations being made to make sure the miners lose this strike? This is not some student demo.'

'Students don't demonstrate nowadays, daddy. You ought to know that. They're far too busy trying to make ends meet and get a good degree.'

'Don't be facetious, honey. You know what I mean. And be careful what you say over the telephone. Those bad lines might signify we're being bugged.'

'You've been reading too many books about the CIA, dad. This is England, not the US.'

'I know,' said Quakke, thinking of some unpleasant experiences he had already undergone in this green and pleasant land. 'All the same. Take care, honey.'

It was sweet of him. Still, as she turned off the motorway and headed for the coking plant at

Pepperidge in her battered white mini, Gemma did have a few misgivings. She had learned from the men outside Grimeford Colliery that they would be providing part of a mass picket at the coking plant and made up her mind that she would get her scoop. In addition to her notebook and small cassette recorder, she had the powerful camera her father had given her for her eighteenth birthday. Some of the men had disturbed her. After all, she wasn't used to working men, even after a time spent in Grimeford. Some of them seemed a bit aggressive. The tall, blonde guy had impressed her, though – perhaps a bit less than rough. She smiled again to herself. The paper had not been too keen on her plans, but, funnily enough, nobody else had volunteered. Another niggling worry which subdued the smile somewhat.

– – –

The Pepperidge plant lay at the end of a long wide avenue of poplars. Behind these, to the right, a large area of wasteground, to the left some derelict factory buildings interspersed with deciduous trees which had seeded themselves a long time ago. All seemed nice and calm. Lorries were coming and going at irregular and well-spaced intervals. About a hundred and fifty miners were positioned, some on one side of the road, others on the other side. There was a police presence of some thirty or so men, with half a dozen on horseback, easing the miners back, when a lorry approached, allowing a few miners to approach lorries coming to the plant with a view to persuading them to turn back and not collect coke.

If, as did happen from time to time, lorries were apparently not going to slow down, the police would try to keep the road clear as the vehicles went through to shouts of 'Scab!', 'Scum!', or 'Traitor!'. Similar shouts would drown the engines of lorries speeding away from the plant. Occasionally miners would have to dive out of the way as some lorries appeared to be unable to slow down sufficiently to avoid them.

'Christ!' swore Billy Cooper as one juggernaut narrowly missed him. 'Have these fuckers got driving licences or what?'

'We've heard that they're using anybody – ex-cons, soldiers, the bloody lot, anybody who's got the bloody nerve and fancies a big fat pay cheque. Most of the lorries haven't even got names on,' said Bill Jones from the Union, out of breath.

'P'raps I'd be better off on their fuckin' side then,' said Billy. 'We're wastin' us fuckin' time here.'

'Pig it, Billy,' shouted Rob Bates further down the line.

Tim had to admit to himself that Billy had a point. Still, at least things hadn't gone as badly as he had thought and he was beginning to enjoy himself. It was something to do, at any rate – better than hanging about his own pit gates where hardly anybody had dared to blackleg as yet.

'Lorry coming,' shouted a policeman as the traffic flow appeared to be increasing. Both miners and police prepared to do what Pin-stripe would have described as their 'several duties'.

Suddenly, as the police got into well-rehearsed positions and joined arms, half a brick struck one of them and he fell to the ground with a thud as a voice – somebody remembered later it did not have a Yorkshire accent – shouted 'Let's get vese bleedin' pigs aht ve way!' One of them was, indeed, bleeding and – what with attempts to maintain the line on the part of the police, attempts on the part of the miners to see who had thrown the missile and attempts from both groups to avoid vehicles which were determined to get through, regardless, a melee broke out in which pushing and shoving, baton-wielding, kicking and punching were all mixed up as the scrum staggered across the road, amid frantically braking and accelerating lorries, and onto the wasteground on the right.

'What the fuck's happenin'?' shouted Tim, as he got separated from the rest of the Grimeford bunch, but good prop forward that he was he got his head down out of the way of flailing truncheons and tried to make for space.

'Hold 'em on the wasteground!' shouted a police inspector. Whistles blew and as the miners were pushed over onto the right many escaped to what they saw as the safety of open space.

It was then that the clatter of hooves was heard as the mounted came across the road from the cover of the trees and onto the wasteground to the front of the fleeing miners. Those who turned back in the other direction now found their escape blocked, not only by the original squad of police, but also by two hundred police in riot gear. Some of the Grimeford lads had picked up a broken telegraph pole, and charging with it, managed to break a way through the riot shields, followed by other groups. Helmeted visors were knocked off, batons seized and used against the police, stones picked up and hurled as the escapees got back to the road and headed for their parked vans and succeeded in preventing pursuit.

'Hey, that's mi twattin' brother-in-law what's supposed to be in the army in friggin' Catterick!' exclaimed Billy, recognising one of the riot police who was vainly trying to pick up his helmet.

'Coom on, yer fuckin' git,' growled Rob at him as he pulled at his sleeve and turned him round. They headed back to the van and got in, locking the doors.

'Wheer's Tim?' said Rob as they did a count. 'Ah'm gooin' back for 'im.'

'Steady on lad,' said Bill Jones, pulling back both Rob and the back door of the van. 'Jim, drive off, then come round again, and we'll pick him up. No point losing anybody else.'

Gemma was trembling all over, but with the same hypnotism by which some snakes paralyse their prey, she was rooted to the spot behind one of the poplars on the right hand side of the road and was continuing to take pictures of miners being ridden down by horses, struck with batons, limping off bleeding in all directions, holding heads, stomachs, legs, other more tender parts of their anatomy. Some of the police were not much better off either and Gemma was surprised to see how ambulances had come on the scene so quickly. Her long, golden hair was pinned up and hidden under a sailor cap and the rest of her clothes were dark so that she remained inconspicuous and, at a pinch, could have passed as a policewoman.

She saw one miner running for his life come past her, pursued at a distance by a mounted officer. As he came level with the tree she saw him stumble, grasp at his leg and go down. The horse was nearly on him and the policeman swinging his baton. Suddenly released from every emotion except pity, Gemma sprang forward and pulled at the man's arm. He was heavy, but not as heavy as the horse which thundered over them, the swinging baton smashing the camera which was still slung around Gemma's neck.

Tim was unclear what was happening. He had been winded when he fell and a searing pain shot up his leg. Now, someone was trying to pull him along the ground and everything was going dark above him. He felt another searing pain as the horse's hoof slashed his ear and he felt blood trickling down his face. Then brightness again and he was heaped on the ground on top of somebody.

'Bloody 'ell, it's you!' he said.

'It is,' said Gemma, unable to think of anything more profound at the moment. 'Come on, I've got the car just up here. We don't need this.' She pulled off the smashed camera and threw it to the ground.

As the transit van came round for the second time, Billy Cooper, keen-eyed as ever, if rather less acute in the brain compartment, spotted two blonde-haired figures slipping into a white mini.

'Yer've nooa need ter worry abaht Tim,' he sighed enviously, 'he's fallen on a bed o' roses ageean.'

'How's your leg?' asked Gemma, as she put a large plaster over Tim's ear. Now it had started to clot, it didn't look quite so bad.

'It'll be reight,' said Tim, who was used to rugby injuries. 'Ah've nobbut twisted it, ah think.'

'Well if it's nobbut twisted...' laughed Gemma, 'let's be gooin' then.'

'Gi' o'er, Jack warned me about you teasers,' he said, wincing. 'Pity you lost the film, though. There must be some good shots on it.'

'Who says I lost the film, then?' replied Gemma, patting a little bulge in her jacket pocket as she released the handbrake and coaxed the little car into life.

– – –

There was a deal of mirth in the Antidiluvian Club as some of its Committee watched shots of the action relayed from the battlefield.

'Just like Caesar at Cannae,' yelped Sir Hugh, whose knowledge of military engagements was somewhat rusty. 'Wipers all over again.'

'At least, so far, Freeman doesn't seem to have gone over the top,' thought Sir Julian, as events unfolded.

'Classic cavalry manoeuvre,' guffawed Sir Hugh, whose own speciality was infantry.

'We shall make sure the film is cut about a bit,' said Lord Slack, 'make it appear as if any police action was merely defensive, a reaction to aggression from the miners. Those lefties in the BBC are taking our footage anyway, so there shouldn't be any trouble there. We'll get plenty of shots in of bricks and bottles striking the horses. That should go down well in the shires.'

'Good idea!' chuckled Sir Hugh, 'man's best friend and all that.'

'Brilliant idea to put the camera in a portaloo, don't you think?' carried on Slack in self-congratulatory mode.

'Quite so,' murmured Kronos, sipping his coffee and reaching for another ginger biscuit to keep his stamina up.

'Hello, what's happened there?' shouted Sir Hugh, as, with a mighty crash and crackle, the picture disappeared.

'Probably hit by one of those bloody great horses,' grumbled Slack, 'never mind. We've got plenty more dotted about. Holy shit! It's gone up in flames!' he exclaimed as another camera switched in.

'Battle of Britain all over again,' put in Sir Duckham, determined that the junior service should have a reference, even if not directly involved. At least his memory was more accurate than Sir Hugh's ancient history. 'Looks like we've got Jerry on the run.'

'Coal miners, Sir Duckham,' reminded a northern Captain of Industry noted for the acuteness of his observation.

'Where?' responded Sir Duckham, looking round as though he feared some abrupt incursion into the Retiring Room of the Antidiluvian Club. 'Oh, yes, quite. Still, good show.'

'Gad, looks like some damned woman there,' expostulated Sir Hugh as he caught sight of a horse jumping a couple of figures huddled on the ground next to the trees.

'Some of these miner chappies have very long hair these days,' explained Sir Duckham, an expert once again. 'Sometimes can't tell the difference meself. Anyway, look he's wearing trousers.'

This was conclusive evidence to Sir Hugh. In the circles in which he moved, ladies did not wear trousers. Sir Julian was less than convinced, however. There was something familiar about the gait, the determination of the long-haired blonde who was dragging his or her companion towards the trees.

'Bloody effeminate,' Sir Duckham carried on. 'Used to have nancy-boys in the RAF, y'know. Made 'em cut their hair, though. Didn't want 'em looking like their mothers.'

'A very good point, if I may say so, Sir Duckham,' smiled Kronos, deciding he didn't need another ginger biscuit and pulling out a cigar. 'A very good point indeed.'

– – –

'Aren't you hungry?' asked Lucy, concerned as Quakke pushed away his half-finished plate of egg and chips and turned off the evening news. 'It's your favourite.'

'I know, sweetie-pie,' sighed Hymer, 'but you saw the newsreels. Miners and police fighting each other. I don't like Gemma being in the middle of all that.'

'You always were a worrier, Hymie,' said Lucy, kissing him reassuringly in a way which might once have led onto other things. He gently squeezed her breast through the thin summer blouse by way of gratitude rather than excitement. She kissed him again. 'Even if she lives in the middle of it, it doesn't mean to say that she's mixed up in it. Nobody would send a junior reporter to cover a story like that. You remember how boring she told you it was – weddings, funerals, Church fetes, all that kind of stuff.'

'Yes, honey, I guess so, but you know what Gemma's like.' He knew her perhaps better than her mother, he thought, having spent most of her life with her. 'She's headstrong, like you, stubborn even, cocky.'

'Now you're talking,' laughed Lucy, slipping her hand beneath his trouser-belt.

'No, leave off, sugar!' said Quakke, wriggling away. Terrible memories of Irma suddenly filled his mind. 'I'm serious about this. I told her to be careful, but I can't be there with her. I have these awful premonitions sometimes.' (As well as memories, he was thinking). 'She's still my baby, you know.'

'Ours, dear,' said Lucy, kissing him reassuringly once more. 'But she doesn't think that way any more. Sure, she loves us, but she's eighteen, she's an adult. She wants to start her own life now.'

'I guess you're right,' said Hymer, not at all convinced. 'She has led a very sheltered life, though.'

'I'd led a sheltered life when I was her age,' laughed Lucy. 'Mostly park shelters and bus shelters.'

'Garn with yer,' said Quakke, slapping her affectionately on the thigh. 'Let's go down the pub.'

It was a time when self-improvement, sufficiency and mastery could go to the dogs. What he needed at the moment was a liberal dose of amnesia.

– – –

'Just putting the paper to bed, boss,' said John Dent, sticking his head round the door of the Editor of "The Grimeford Gazette". Harry Keene knocked back another hay-fever tablet, swigged a glass of weak whisky and water and muttered, 'I think you'd be better occupied putting me to bed.' He wiped his streaming nose on a tissue, man-size, and lobbed it towards the wastepaper basket in the corner. He could have had it next to his desk, but it amused him to see how often he could get screwed-up balls of paper, or latterly, tissues, into it from six yards. For the seventh time out of as many last attempts the soggy mass hit the rim of the basket and floundered on the floor. Seven was definitely not a magic number for him. The misses only served to remind him what a rotten few hours he had been having.

'Best offer I've had all day, Harry,' said John, cheerfully.

'Don't be bloody facetious,' grunted Keene. 'Save it for the Friday column. You know what I mean, I've been struggling with this hay-fever for four days now. Whether it's the oil seed rape or what. These tablets are no bloody good, either. All I want to do at the moment is get home, get a few whiskies down me and into the Land of Nod.' He flung the pill-bottle towards the wastepaper basket, missing again.

'Don't you want to see what we've got then?'

'No thanks, you're the Sub-Editor, go and bloody sub-edit.'

'It's just that some stuff brought in from Pepperidge by that lass, well, I think it could be a scoop.'

'What, little miss hoity-toity Quakkers? Give us a break, John. It's been on the tele, ITV have scooped it. Bloody miners misbehaving again. What's new?'

'Steady, Harry. My dad was a miner.'

'An' look what he got from misbehavin'! Provincial newspapers don't get scoops nowadays. The last time anybody here got a chance was 1912 when the Titanic went down and it appeared on page 5 as "Grimeford man dies at sea". Just get it out, John. I'm off home to bed.'

'She thinks it was a set-up job. In fact, she thinks the whole strike was a set-up job and that things are going to get worse before they get better.'

'A lot of miners think it was a set-up job, hasn't your dad told yer? A lot of Nottingham miners think Arthur set it up – and cocked it up for that matter. You can't close coking plants like you could ten years ago. And if I don't go home now and get

133

some brown medicine down me this hay-fever is going to get worse before it gets better.'

'You shouldn't drink and take tablets, Harry.'

'And who are you, then, my bleeding nanny?'

'No, I was just saying...'

'Well, go and say it to somebody else, otherwise I shan't be home before 2 o'clock. Publish and be damned, lad, publish and be damned.'

'Front page, then?'

'If yer like. All we had before was councillors off to Russia on free junketings. We didn't exactly have much proof on that one, either.'

'What about the photographs?'

'Phu...choo? Phu...choo? Photographs?' Usually when Harry started with one of his sneezing fits it went on for at least twenty-seven times. However, on this occasion, surprise must have cut off his tickle at source. 'Keep you and this lass on and I could sack the rest of the bloody staff – photographers and all!'

'Her dad gave her a camera.'

'That's it,' snapped Keene. 'That is bloody it. PhD theses and frigging Kodak Brownie pictures. I am definitely going home now. If anything develops,' a momentary snigger, 'if anything develops, don't wake me. When I think I could once have had a job on the "Yorkshire Po... choo... choo... choo...' The attack this time was destined to go its full course, and Keene stamped off down the corridor, stopping only after sneeze twenty-seven to yell back 'Publish and be damned!' and 'See you in the dole queue, John.'

Chapter Five

'Well, I'll be damned,' breathed Harry Keene as, relatively refreshed after his night's sleep and the hay-fever much improved, he scanned the front page of "The Grimeford Gazette". 'Well, I'll be damned.' It was as near to speechless as he ever got.

The front page was plastered with pictures of mounted policemen lurking in the old industrial estate on the left of the plant, of riot police without identification numbers, of horses being ridden full tilt at unarmed miners, of limping, bleeding casualties. The text bore reference to the inauthenticity of the 'miner' who had thrown the first brick, to the tactics of the police who were expecting to trap the miners on the wasteground and to concealed television cameras which were obviously relaying events back to some operations room. All this, allied to the fact that so many miners had been allowed to arrive at the plant, when previously road-blocks had prevented most of them even leaving their villages argued strongly that a show-down, an OK Corral situation had been planned. Gemma also linked this in with the preparations, the coal movements she had observed prior to the strike, collieries closed without going through the normal review period and deliberate provocations during the overtime ban. Quakke and Dent had done a good job.

Keene still felt he had to watch his back, though, especially when the Chairman of the group to which the "Gazette" belonged burned his ear for ten minutes on the responsibilities of an Editor. However, when the story and the pictures were syndicated to every national daily and weekly, thence to the USA and the Eastern Block and the paper generated more money than it had in the total of its hundred years' existence, a sober note of congratulation reached him.

– – –

'Well, I'll be damned,' breathed Sir Julian Callendar. He was in the habit of receiving all the newspapers although the story was so universal he only needed one. 'So that's what the little minx was up to!' He was waiting for his two former colleagues in ARE who made up the Inner Cabinet of the Antidiluvian Club.

'Who's responsible for this then?' asked Freeman, as he arrived before his female colleague.

'You remember Lucy Lastick, don't you?'

'Oh yes, I remember Lucy alright,' guffawed Fritzy. 'Nice bit of cunt she was.'

'Yes, well, you also remember, I'm sure, that she married that nutty American professor that we screwed up. Thought he might be on to you at one time, but we managed to put him off the scent. This is their daughter Gemma, reporting for some tin-pot rag in the coalfields.'

'Well, vis report's got a bit furver!' exclaimed Freeman, lapsing into the vernacular. 'We don't want people like that cocking fings up for us, do we? Looks to me as vough she needs seeing to.'

'I think not – morning, Julie,' said Callendar as the beautiful dark-skinned girl entered the room. 'I think this is one of those times when we sight and think about changing tack. There are one or two interesting developments coming on line,' he looked at Julie, who continued, 'As far as the reactions to this are concerned,' she slapped the back of her hand on the front page of the "Gazette", 'I don't think we need worry too much.'

'The public are already persuaded that the miners' leadership is deranged and undemocratic. There are no power cuts, no three day weeks. Working miners will, no doubt, be grateful that the police are so effective in keeping coal production flowing and in dealing with pickets, thereby implying more protection for them. I imagine we can safely discount any adverse reaction in the USA. They love hard-nosed industrial relations. As for the Eastern Block. It might keep churning out a few thousands for the strike fund, but it is basically moving towards being an outsize version of Sicily.'

'You have, of course, played a large part yourself in helping to organise women's support groups,' emphasized Sir Julian.

'I have,' continued Julie, 'and I think these have managed to take some heat out of the situation, as well as allowing the strike to go on for as long as we want it.'

'Thank you, Julie,' smiled Callendar. 'I mentioned changing tack. We hear from Nottingham that some working miners are thinking of challenging the legality of a strike called without a national ballot. The Government has made laws, of course, which would allow for the sequestration of Union funds in the case of an illegal strike - but has so far, on our advice of course – refrained from using them. We now think it would be worthwhile to support the working miner a bit more, get the legal fees of these chappies paid for, organise some meetings to encourage those already working and encourage more back to work. We have a fairly substantial commitment from Monty Hawk, you know the video king, and we might even set up public subscriptions. The court case will succeed, it goes without saying, but we shan't get hold of any money. It will already have disappeared somewhere. It's the publicity that counts. Meet again in a few weeks then.'

Sir Fritzy Freeman shot off to attend to his beloved soccer team which had a European Cup tie that evening, but not before muttering what sounded like 'Me brain 'urts. Direct action. Direct action.'

– – –

'I'm surprised that your story died down so quick,' said Tim, trying to come over with his best CSE grade 1 English. 'Still, I suppose bottom line is, nobody cares about us bug...'

'You can swear if you like. I don't mind,' laughed Gemma. 'I know what you mean, though. It's as if somebody has decided to ignore it. Is that wounded pride or my suspicious mind again, do you think? I think I got it off dad. There was a nasty business involving my mum, just before I was born, and I guess that changed his attitude to things. He's always telling me to watch my step.'

Tim didn't know. In fact he had not yet recovered from the shock that Gemma was prepared to have a drink with him. As his mates had said, she was in a different class from the girls he could usually pick up on a Saturday night. Nothing wrong with them, but Gemma was special, more interesting, more challenging. Her tight, ribbed sweater, her short skirt and her tights were all black and with her camel jacket, her patent leather shoes with the little chain across and her gold crucifix, her golden hair and her fair complexion were beautifully complemented, Tim thought.

'You look nice tonight,' he said sheepishly.

'Thanks,' smiled Gemma, blushed slightly and looked down at her drink. Quakke was right. Sexually, as well as socially, Gemma was, as yet, quite inexperienced.

'Do you want another?' he asked. He had been drinking quickly, mainly out of embarrassment.

'No thanks. I'll get you one, though,' said Gemma, making to get up.

'No, no,' said Tim, gently restraining her. Short of money he might be, but he wasn't going to let anybody see he couldn't buy a lady a drink. Some old-fashioned codes and courtesies still lingered in the Grimeford Welfare.

'So, your dad's a professor, then?' Tim asked when he got back from the bar, emboldened by another swig of John Smith's. 'What of?'

'It's sort of socio-linguistics,' replied Gemma.

'Socio-what?' said Tim.

Gemma laughed. 'I don't understand it much myself,' she said, lying, then, 'it's to do with how people's speech and behaviour are related.'

'You mean people tell you one thing and then go and do another.'

'A bit like that,' said Gemma.

'And what about you, what will you be studying like?'

'PPE. Politics, Philosophy, and Economics.'

'You've made a good start on the first any road up.'

'Maybe,' laughed Gemma, 'maybe not.'

'I suppose you'll meet plenty of lads down there in Oxford. More your own sort, you know.'

'Maybe,' laughed Gemma, 'maybe not.' She was shaking her hair back into position, slightly embarrassed. Actually it was Tim's embarrassment which was getting to her. She wished he would just try to be himself. She tried to lighten the situation again. 'Actually, the college I'm going to only takes women. Somebody told me if you had any male visitors in your room you had to wheel the bed outside. I don't know whether they still have that rule.'

'You could still do it on the floor, though, couldn't you?' Tim suggested helpfully. The momentary pause and the faraway look in his eyes suggested he might be imagining Gemma spread out naked on a large lambskin rug in front of a roaring fire – coal of course. He'd pass up the offer of tea and muffins.

'Penny for them,' said Gemma, calling him back to the noisy reality of a South Yorkshire drinking club.

'Oh, well, ar... I was just trying to remember this joke. Something about a couple who always ended up on the floor when they had a... made love like, because they liked a matt finish.'

This tickled Gemma. She liked jokes with puns in and they both laughed.

It broke the ice. Tim told her about his family, about his hopes for the future, about his mates, even when asked, about some of the girls he'd been out with, but then Gemma changed the subject, not wishing to admit to her own inexperience. She told him about her dad, her mum, about the gap still in her understanding of what had happened to her mum in prison, although she knew it couldn't have been her fault. She was such an innocent sort of person herself, as indeed was Gemma.

'Do you think some people are natural victims?' asked Tim. 'And the opposite, of course, natural oppressors.' She was suddenly surprised at the acuteness of the question, although she had realised he was intelligent. 'I suppose you might have to practise a bit, as well, to keep it up, I mean.'

Tim got some more drinks. It had been worth the ignominy of scrounging a few bob from his elder brother who was an accountant in Doncaster. He was just returning to the table when a police officer approached it amid sneers and boos and cat calls.. He ignored them.

'Excuse me, miss, are you the owner of that white mini outside? Some lads have just put a brick through the window. We've been chasin 'em about all night, bloody hooligans.'

'What a nuisance,' said Gemma, to whom it seemed no more than that.

'If you'd just step outside for a mo' then and get it reported you'll be able to claim it on your insurance. You can 'ardly 'ear yourself speak in 'ere,' he shouted above the jeers which were continuing and the music which the DJ had thoughtfully turned up. 'I'll come an' all,' said Tim, snatching a quick drink out of his pint and wiping the froth off with the back of his hand.

Gemma went out first, with the policeman. As he came through the door of the Welfare, Tim noticed two 'officers' next to a plain van. He had only time to shout out, 'Look out, Gemma, they've no numbers on!' before he felt a sickening crack on his shoulder and he went down. Gemma was bundled into the back of the van which, with squealing clutch, shot off towards the main road.

'You're going to enjoy vis, luv,' snarled the man who was holding Gemma by the arms as another 'officer' tried to pull off her tights. 'Yer mum always used to. Lav'ly fack she was.' Gemma didn't understand the reference to the past, but what was going on at the moment was all too clear. In desperation she bit hard on the hand which held her, kicked out with her feet and lunged for the back of the van.

The vans used for these covert operations were not Mercedes, as well as having numberplates obscured by an (accidental?) accumulation of greasy dirt, they had an appreciable percentage of rust. What went through Gemma's mind as the back doors of the van gave way and she hurtled into the path of an unmarked juggernaut sneaking coal out of the pit under cover of darkness, if anything, in that split second could, is perhaps best left to the imagination.

'I couldn't avoid her,' said the lorry driver to the 'officers' from the van. 'There was no way I could have avoided her.'

'S'awright mate,' the elder of the four 'policemen' reassured the trembling wreck in front of him. 'Just one of vose fings. Pretty slippery customer vat,' he continued, gesturing towards the tangled mess which still lay in the road from which the lorry-driver quickly averted his gaze again. 'Alky, druggie, tea-leaf... you mention it. Better off wivout vat sort, eh mate? Just give us yer particulars and we'll sort the rest out.'

'Yeah, well, alright,' mumbled the driver, getting back into his cab and coming back with his licence, his insurance, and his tachogram. Logos passed these onto one of his colleagues who made some notes, but not without an inward sigh of relief. This guy was not a real lorry-driver, but one of those cowboys and his tacho showed he had been driving too long without a break. Even if he was surprised at being called to an inquest, he would not be in a hurry to come forward and risk prosecution.

'You'll be hearing from us, mate,' said Logos to the man who was trembling even more now he thought his cover had been blown.

'What about...?' he started.

'I said we'd 'andle it. mate...awright,' cut in the other. 'Get back in the cab and move that bloody great heap of scrap, pronto.' The driver shrugged. This was the police after all. They knew what they were doing, he supposed. He took a deep breath and pulled away. If it had been a dusty evening, one would have not seen him for it.

'I don't like this at all, guv,' moaned one of the two men in front of the van.

'You was paid fer dirty work,' Logos reminded him, 'and dirty work you got.'

'Not this dirty,' complained the 'officer'.

'Well, yer got it now, ain't cher? Let's get a move on. Get her in ver back of ver van. Vat's it. Dave's follerin' in the mini. We'll transfer her to vat, take it somewhere quiet, run it off ver road, an' set fire to it.'

The 'real' police were alerted next morning to the fact that a burnt-out mini was lying in a field off a sharp bend on a quiet country road outside Doncaster. It had evidently gone out of control, left the road and burst into flames. There were no streetlamps on that stretch and the car was beyond the range of headlights, especially as the corner was turned, so no one had spotted it any earlier. The body of a young female, identifiable only by her bone structure and dental records was extracted by the Fire Brigade. The number plate of the car, an old-fashioned one with raised numbers, tied in with the identity and next of kin were informed.

''As she ditched thee, then?' Rob had said to Tim as he staggered back into the Welfare.

'No, look,' Tim said in a daze and with a total feeling of weakness in his right arm. 'She's been picked up by the fuzz.'

'An' swung round by the tits a time or two, I shouldn't wonder,' jibed Billy Cooper.

'Shut yer fuckin' gob,' warned Rob, then turning again to Tim.

'What's happened to thi bloody arm?'

'Dunno, somebody hit me on t' shoulder.'

'Lift thi arm,' said Rob, who was in the First Aid and Rescue teams. Tim tried, but immediately let out an agonising yelp.

'Tha's broken thi collar-bone,' said Rob, 'Come on, I'll tek thi to Casualty.'

'What about Gemma?' muttered Tim, through gritted teeth.

'She's probably got sorted out by now,' said Rob as they got into the car-park. The mini's gone anyway. We told thi not ter get mixed up wi' 'er.'

'She's not like that,' said Tim. 'She wouldn't have gone without saying anything. I tell yer, two pigs shoved her in the back of a van. I remember now, I shouted they hadn't any ID.'

'Well, there's not much you can do for 'er now – or anybody else for that matter. Hospital for you, sunshine. Give the paper a ring in the mornin' if y're worried abaht 'er.'

Tim had had to acquiesce.

– – –

When he phoned the paper next morning no one had seen Gemma, no one had heard from Gemma. By the time the local news was on tea-time television, everyone knew what had happened. Freeman received a call to the Antidiluvian Club. Sir Julian Callendar was waiting for him in the smoking-room, chewing a cigar he was too agitated to light. Not only did he have enough humanity in him not to want a second life-stealing experience to happen to Lucy, of whom he had always been fond, even if he had been prepared to use her, but also he was beginning to worry about his own position. All those years ago Pin-stripe had warned him about Logos. During all those years he had striven, successfully as it happened, to keep him under control. Now this.

'You've really done it this time, haven't you?' he hissed at Freeman. 'I thought we'd agreed that there was no other contribution needed on your part at the moment. But you just couldn't keep out of it, could you, had to have your gratuitous 'bit of fun', didn't you?'

'You an' Kaki agreed, vat's ver point. I'm fed up wiv takin' orders from you. Wanted to do a bit of my own direct action for a change.'

'Unless you're very lucky,' snarled Sir Julian, 'we could all be in for a change. There's plenty of people, even whom we consider our friends at the moment who will be only too happy to ditch us, call up some previous misdemeanours, make up some new ones, get us put away for the rest of our lives. I thought you knew that.'

'You never discussed it wiv me, Kronnie boy. You never really discussed anything wiv me, did yer?'

'Certain matters were perhaps beyond your comprehension,' said Sir Julian, regaining his composure.

'You mean I'm fick, don't cher?'

'I didn't say that,' parried Kronos, 'but since you mention it, it doesn't take the IQ of a brain-damaged flea to see that killing off a reporter who has caused us even a small amount of embarrassment is the tactic of a lunatic.'

'Oh, so now I'm a lunatic brain-damaged flea, am I?' grunted Logos, summarising, then, calmer, and almost with regret, 'we didn't mean to kill her. It was an accident.'

'On the Queen's highway. There'll have to be an inquest, you know.'

'The car was duff. We fixed the subframe. We set fire to it. There's hardly enough evidence of her left, let alone the car. Nobody'll know she was dead when we put her in the car.'

'How do you mean, when you put her in the car? What was going on, then?'

'We wus larkin' abaht wiv 'er in the back of the van...'

'Hold on a minute, you mean sexually assaulting her?'

'Yeah, well, I seem to remember when you was younger...'

'Promiscuous, I may have been, but sexual assault – never,' spluttered Callendar.

'Alright, then Mr High and Mighty, we wus... sexually assaultin' 'er in the back of the van, when she got loose an' fell aht the back door into the path of a lorry.'

'So there's a lorry driver involved?'

'Yeah, but don't worry, 'e was a moonlightin' blackleg. You won't find 'im comin' forward in a 'urry.'

'What about blood on the road?'

'Well, we obviously didn't have no mop an' bucket wiv us, but there was a right downpour soon afterwards. Probably cleaned up alright.'

'We can do without the humour, thank you very much, Freeman,' said Sir Julian. 'I am still unclear about what this girl was doing in the van in the first place.'

'We picked 'er up.'

'That would be theorematic,' sneered Callendar. 'What I mean is where did you pick her up?'

'At the Miner's Welfare, she was there wiv some miner trog. We had to give him a bit of a whack.'

'What!' Sir Julian exploded, 'You picked her up in a place full of potentially hostile witnesses and abducted her. The police are going to have a field day with that.'

'We were the police, I mean we were dressed as police. Didn't 'ave any numbers on vough.'

'You cretin,' yelled Callendar, 'you bloody cretin, that makes it worse. Somebody will have noticed that.'

'Well that git she wus wiv did I fink. It was the last fing he said before we 'it 'im. We could always go and do 'im over...'

'Enough! Enough!' shouted Callendar, purple-faced. Just keep out of the way for a bit. I suppose we shall have to try and cover your tracks, but believe me, when this thing's over...'

Freeman did not need to wait for the missing words, he wasn't that stupid.

He said to himself as he left the Antidiluvian Club. 'Yes an' if I'm finished Kronnie Boy, I take you wiv me!'

Chapter Six

Tim spent some uncomfortable nights whilst he got used to the sling around his right arm which meant he couldn't sleep on his side as he usually did. When he was not in pain from the bone starting to knit, he was fuzzy-headed from the pain-killers. As he got about a bit and had managed to grin at the hundredth reference to his having to use his left hand instead, nudge, nudge, wink, wink, the incapacity became more of an inconvenience that would take its time to pass over, probably about five weeks. Fortunately Rob was able to take him about a bit in the car.

When Tim's head cleared he started to put things into perspective. An attempt to interest the police in a story of kidnapping and murder had not borne fruit. He was the only witness and even with a broken collar-bone was not going to overcome single-handedly the mutual suspicion which existed between the miners and the guardians of the peace. The reference to four, possibly five policemen being at the Welfare on the night in question was treated with derision – 'We only had two men on duty in the whole of Grimeford that night, lad.' As for the allegations of unidentifiable officers – 'Oh, that old tale again', then 'Look, lad, we know you'll be upset at losing your friend, but it won't do any good going over and over it. It were an accident, pure and simple. Just try and accept that and get over it.' No, if any sense were to be made of what had happened to Gemma, he would have to do it himself. He wrote to Quakke, care of Lanchester University, saying that he was a friend of Gemma's and that he would like to attend the funeral, nothing more at the moment. Rob wrote the letter at his dictation, actually, with constant 'How do yer spell's' because Tim couldn't write with his left hand.

The Inquest was a perfunctory affair. The mini had been thoroughly examined and the tread on three of the tyres found to be inconsistent with safe road-holding as well as the sub-frame coming apart. The wet road, the unlit corner and Gemma's lack of experience as a driver were all held to be contributory factors.

'Funny,' thought Tim, 'I'm sure she told me after Pepperidge she'd just had three new tyres. I was joking about the mini not getting us back to Grimeford.'

He had had a shock on entering the room set aside in the Magistrates Court to see what he thought was Gemma in the front row. He felt his stomach churn, although he quickly realised it was her mother who at forty-odd was still stunning enough to turn heads. The distinguished, if slightly vague man sitting next to her was, he supposed, Hymer Quakke.

'P'raps I ought to go and have a word,' Tim whispered to Rob as the Inquest broke up.

'Ah should leave it fer now, mate,' replied Rob, glancing at the weeping Lucy being helped out by a sad, but determined-looking Quakke.

Media coverage was equally perfunctory. Reference was made to the Coroner's regret at the sad loss of a young life and his warning to newly-qualified drivers on vehicle maintenance and excessive speed was emphasized, but there were other things in the news. A spate of Loyalist marches in Northern Ireland was generating fear of a fresh outbreak of violence, miners were drifting back to work, especially now it appeared the Union would be sued over its failure to hold a national ballot, and the Chairman of Chesterham United had resigned, taking with him his entire investment, and causing a crisis on the board.

As the tall, dark man in the pin-striped suit was comforting Lucy, expressing his regret that he wouldn't have time to come back to the house for the light refreshments which had been laid on for mourners travelling a distance, Tim took the opportunity to speak to Quakke.

'Tim Glasby,' he said, offering his left hand to Quakke. 'I wrote to you, remember?'

'Yes, of course,' said Quakke, 'good of you to come.'

'And this is Rob Bates.'

'Howdy.' Quakke proffered his right hand to the physically intact member of the duo. 'Are you coming back to the house? You've come a long way.'

'Yes, I should like to have a word with you,' confided Tim in a half-whisper, feeling suddenly uneasy as the dark man talking to Lucy glanced quickly in their direction.

'Let's go then,' said Quakke. 'Honey!' he called out to Lucy as the pin-striped Civil Servant climbed into his chauffeur-driven Daimler and waved goodbye. 'Guys, this is my wife.'

'I can tell,' burbled Tim while Quakke continued 'Lucy, meet Tim and Rob.'

Together they went through the Lych gate of the churchyard of Listerham-on-Severn and made for the thatched cottage opposite.

'Do you like the country, boys?' asked Quakke, trying to make polite conversation.

'We 'avent much experience of it, 'ave we Tim?' said Rob.

– – –

What surprised Tim most, as he sat in Quakke's study, was that the latter wasn't – surprised that is – to learn of the young miner's suspicions about Gemma's death. As he listened to the tale of abduction, Quakke recognised a familiar pattern. At his age, though, was it another opportunity to bring to justice the instigators of foul deeds or simply another chapter of sadness and frustration he would have to force to the back of his mind? He told him all he knew about the Tolbridge affair and Lucy's involvement in it.

'What motive would anybody have to cause those two deaths, then?' asked Tim.

'I don't know,' replied Quakke, 'that's the beauty of it from their point of view. They would be motiveless, I suppose – recreational.'

'You mean pure bloody sadism?'

'You could say that, I guess.'

'And you think the same people are behind Gemma's death? Does that mean it's somebody who's got it in for you – or Lucy?'

'Can't see why.' Quakke shrugged his shoulders and reached for his Bourbon on the rocks. 'Anyway, Ernest was a friend but he had nothing to do with his really.'

'And Gemma?'

'From what you've told me it looks as though somebody was taking revenge on Gemma for that report on the Battle of Pepperidge.'

'Like who? The bobbies, the Government, the working miners? Seems a bit on the heavy side to me. The story soon died down, you know.'

'I know,' said Quakke who had been relieved about it at the time. 'Post hoc sed non propter hoc.'

'You've lost me there,' said Tim.

'No direct consequence,' continued Quakke, 'but suppose her efforts in the press drew her to the attention of some perverted…'

'Sadist?' put in Rob.

'Or suppose,' Quakke went on, 'it was a direct consequence and things got out of hand.'

'Still the same murderous thugs, though.'

'Precisely,' concluded Quakke. 'Anyway, I must go and see what's going on out there now. Keep in touch. Come and see me again, but no phone calls. Buggers.'

'Aye, there's plenty of them about,' sighed Tim.

− − −

Whilst what Quakke had told Tim and Rob about Tolbridge had been very interesting and perhaps warned him of the opposition he was up against, there were no details he could take as practical starting points. There were not even any typed notes or men with chameleonic hair to take into account. He would have to start from what he knew himself:

A policeman asked Gemma to step outside. Did he have an identification number or not? Tim couldn't remember, he had not noticed at the time. Probably not. No one who had been in the Welfare that night knew who he was. He was probably not local.

The 'officer' knew what car Gemma was driving. They could have watched her arrive or have seen her in it beforehand. Perhaps even at the coking plant.

The 'officers' outside the Welfare were definitely unidentifiable. Tim had shouted this out just before he got hit on the shoulder.

There was a white van. Two 'officers' grabbed hold of Gemma and had been about to put her in the van when he had lost consciousness. Did they rough her up a bit in the van then shove her in her own car and tell her to get lost? If so where was she heading when she went off the road? Or did they take her off in the van with another 'officer' driving the car? That seemed more likely. They wouldn't want to hang about outside the Welfare. In which case, how did she get into her own car and, as before, where was she going in it? Why didn't she come back to the Welfare? If she'd been given one fright, and maybe a warning, they wouldn't be coming to look for her there again. If she had been dumped on the narrow country road, she would have had to be heading in the opposite direction even to get home. Reluctantly Tim came to the conclusion that when Gemma was transferred to the mini she was already dead.

What was it Quakke had said? What if things had gone wrong? What if the roughing up got too rough? Tim forced himself not to think about that, but he had now reached an impasse. He had a good idea of what had happened, but how and who...?

– – –

No detective can manage without a stroke of luck. His powers of observation may be acute – he may be able to tell at a glance, perhaps, that a man has had a bacon sandwich for breakfast – his powers of deduction may rival those of Descartes himself, but without luck and/or the carelessness of the criminal, he is nothing.

Tim's luck came one Friday evening towards the end of September. Rob and he had decided to give the Welfare a miss and go for a quiet drink at "The Slater's Arms". It was an old pub, a drinker's pub where there was no music, no bar snacks, no microwaved "evening meals", no pool tables, no darts, no women, well... not unless you counted old Betty and her mate from down the road who spent all evening playing beggar my neighbour in the snug over a couple of halves of milk stout. There was no sawdust on the floor now, but as a concession to the passage of time the old spittoons were repositories for potted plants, the sort that need no light and grow no flowers. Tim and Rob knew the landlord, a decent sort of chap who was holding out as long as he could against the brewery who wanted to change the establishment into a theme pub. It was a bit, Rob used to say, like the Coal Board. Most of the collieries would soon be theme parks.

'Hello, lads, 'aven't seen youse fer some time nah, slummin' it terneet are yer?' asked the landlord with cheerful self-denigration. 'Two pints, is it?'

'Aye, that'll do, Dave,' said Rob, 'e's payin'', he jerked a thumb towards Tim.

'Ah thought it were thy turn,' grumbled Tim, paying up all the same.

'Who carted thee abaht all that time tha were bad wi' thi arm,' chirped Rob. 'Nah tha's getten thi sling off, that can start gerrin' me a few o' them tha owes me.'

'Reight enough,' said Tim, only too glad to have something to celebrate, though his arm was not exactly much use yet.

'Quiet, toneet,' observed Rob. He was already a quarter way down his first pint before Tim got his change.

'Aye,' said Dave, 'there's nobbut t' bathing beauties an' yon' miserable sod I' t' back 'oil.' He jerked his hand in the direction of the back room of the pub which didn't really merit description as anything else but a hole.

'Who's that then,' asked Tim.

'Ted Harrison, he's bin in iv'ry neet lately. Keeps crying to hissen, then falls asleep.'

'Ah should think 'e does, the scabby bastard,' exploded Rob, "E's been back down four weeks now and I heard 'e were drivin' lorries at neet an' all. He were drivin' 'em all day before 'e went back.'

"E 'as got seven kids, Rob.' Tim was in a conciliatory mood.

'Miners' Support, Tim, Miners' Support. He's not t' only one in that position. Anyway, he should 'ave been moor bloody careful. Specially if any on 'em turn aht like him.'

'Can't you refuse to serve scabs?' asked Tim, rapidly going off him.

'Wi' my relations wi' t' Brewery? Oh aye,' said Dave, scoffing. 'As long as 'e pays, an' 'e does seem to 'ave plenty o' money at t' moment, an' as long as he causes no bother, which he dun't, I can't refuse to serve him.'

'We'd better 'ave a word wi' 'im, then,' said Rob.

'Ah don't want no trouble,' said Dave, 'that'd be just what t' Brewery wants.'

'You know us, Dave,' Tim reassured him.

'Aye, 'appen,' said Dave, nervously polishing a glass.

– – –

'What's up then, Ted?' asked Rob, sitting down and pushing a double whisky towards Ted who downed it in one gulp. Took a swig from a half-empty (some might have described it as a half-full) pint and blew hard on his coal-black handkerchief.

'Ah didn't kill 'er,' said Ted, merely continuing the dialogue already going on in his mind. 'It wa'nt my fault. She just fell aht in front o' me.' He didn't know who he was talking to. He didn't care. It was just a relief to get it off his chest

'Who's that, then, Ted?' asked Tim hardly believing his ears, but totally believing his fears.

'That reporter lass. Ah didn't know it were 'er then, mind. They said it were a druggie, a pro', a criminal, summat like that.'

'Who's they?' asked Tim gently, but inwardly excited, then to Rob. 'This lad looks like he could do wi' another drink.' He pulled a fiver out of his shirt pocket.

'Gu steady!' warned Rob.

160

'Just an odd un,' hissed Tim, 'socio linguistics,'

'What!' said Rob, but went, as requested, to the bar.

'Who's they?' repeated Tim with more impatience than he had intended.

'The fuzz, the pigs in the van.'

'It were a pig van were it then, Ted?' teased Rob, coming back with the whisky, which this time, Ted ignored.

'Stop pissin' abaht, yer twat,' snarled Tim. 'Leave this to me.'

'Ther' were four on 'em,' said Ted. 'Took me licence, took me details. Ah wor brickin'. The whole fuckin' lot were out of order. They said they'd be seein' me later. Ah wor brickin'.

'Tha can start brickin' nah an' all,' said Rob.

'Coool it,' warned Tim. 'What were you doin' there in a bloody lorry at that time o' neet?'

'Ah... ah... ah... were doin' a bit o' drivin'' was all Harrison could come up with at short notice and full of beer and whisky.

'Tha were doin' a bit o' moonleetin', blackleggin'',' sneered Rob. 'Come on, iv'rybody's heard abaht thee.'

'Aye well. Ah've got seven kids.'

'Tha had to be good at summat, tha useless fuckin' pillock,' shouted Rob.

'Rob, just come an' watch t' bar for ten minutes while I go fer a crap,' shouted Dave. It was probably crucial to the whole investigation.

'Any road, you 'it 'er,' emphasized Tim.

'She came out o' the back o' the van. Ah couldn't avoid 'er. They told me they'd see to it. Ah didn't know it were 'er till I saw 'er picture in t' paper. Bonny lass she wor.'

'Er, what was she like?' said Tim, gulping, but knowing he had to ask.

'She were a mess.' Harrison downed his whisky again. 'She were definitely dead, but she looked a mess what with 'er tights around 'er ankles an' 'er knickers down... Could I 'ave another whisky, please, lads?'

'Bastards! Bastards! Fuckin' bastards!,' Tim said, but to himself. Things were getting worse. He went to fetch the whisky himself to calm himself down.

'And when nobody called you to an inquest?'

'Ah wasn't too bothered, like – everything being illegal an' wot not. But then the money started comin'.

'What money?' asked Rob, who had just returned.

'Ah don't know where it comes from. I just get it once a week franked first class from London. It's like I'm bein' paid for killin' 'er. Ah'm not that sort of a bloke.'

'Yer a fuckin' wanker,' said Rob, sticking a finger practically up Harrison's nose.

''Ardly!' exclaimed Tim, glad of some light relief. 'Where did the accident happen, then, Ted?'

'Just before that roundabout goin' out of town,' said Ted, feeling relieved he had not much more information to give. 'Where you turn left to go down to t' Racecourse.'

'One more thing, Ted,' said Tim, 'an' then you can buy us a drink. Did these rozzers have any numbers on them?'

'That were t' last thing on mi mind,' burped Ted, 'but one of 'em 'ad a cockney accent.'

With that, he fell asleep.

Kronos had become more and more convinced that what had been an unshakeable, albeit holy, trinity was finished.

'Two's company,' he murmured to Kaki as he left her lush pink lips and travelled orally up towards the dusky navel pierced with a single gold ring. As he kissed her taut breasts Kaki was in no mood for argument, even if she had wanted to disagree.

'He's been sending the lorry driver money. If that's his interpretation of keeping a low profile, he really has gone off his trolley, fallen off his perch,' grunted Kronos between kisses.

'You mean he's an ex-parrot,' giggled Kaki, then winced slightly as one of his kisses turned into a bite on the nipple.

'Soon will be,' said Kronos confidently, 'if I have anything to do with it.'

'What are you going to do? Cut off his bollocks and throw them in the Thames?'

'Certainly not,' laughed Kronos, adjusting his own tackle so that his penis entered her with one thrust which made her gasp. 'I couldn't be sure that I'd thrown away the right bit.'

Kaki giggled again as she began to move her hips in a circular movement, sucking at the dark man, lubricating his movements.

'No,' continued Kronos, 'you know my methods by now. When I say "if I have anything to do with it" I mean "nobody must know I had anything to do with it".'

'That's more like it,' said Kaki, out of breath. 'Who can you get to do it, though? He has a lot of friends of the sort who could do the dirty work. More than you, in fact.'

'I wasn't thinking of a professional,' hissed Kronos, quickening his movements. 'Somebody innocent would do nicely. Remember the Tolbridge affair? Somebody who, with a little help...' he shuddered as Kaki helped herself to another couple of inches and they lay together panting.

'You don't mean Lucy again, surely?' asked Kaki, lighting them both a Black Russian.

'No, I am very fond of Lucy, in spite of what you might think from that other business. I thought she'd only get a year or two supended at the most. Just her luck to come up against Mr Judge bloody hanging Jefferies. Lucy has suffered enough, especially with her daughter going like that.'

'Quakke's too old. Besides he wasn't too hot on the detective work last time.'

'I think he's improved a bit in that department,' said Kronos, 'and I have a feeling he's not on his own now. There's a couple of strong young guys he was talking to at Gemma's funeral. En tout cas, my brown angel, since Loggie boy,' he sneered visibly, 'since Loggie is enjoying an extended break in the Caribbean, we have plenty of time to think how we might, as it were, speed up the course of justice. Sooner or later, of course, that snivelling lorry driver is going to get found out. Not by the Law, it goes without saying. We've stitched that one up alright. But you can't hide much in a little coal town. Spending big money during a coal strike tends to attract attention. However, even when those likely lads find out what really happened they're going to be at a dead end. We shall have to set up a little treasure hunt for them.'

'Sounds like time for a celebration to me,' said Kaki.

'Champagne?'

'I think we'll keep it on ice,' said Kronos. 'For the moment this will do nicely.' He breathed as he slid his hand gently between the beautiful dark woman's legs.'

– – –

Quakke was writing in his diary:

'Days mean very little to me at the moment. With the death of my baby at least half of me has gone to the grave. I might just as well mark any entries from now on with the names of fruit or animals.'

'Banana'

'I wish I were young again. Not so much that the young seem to have less fear. Rather that, generally, they are better at maintaining hope. Is there hope because there is life? Or is life dependent on hope? I have so little of my own. Apart from the comfort of my beautiful wife, nothing gives me pleasure any more. If those young guys could just give me some of their hope, create for me some peace of mind.'

It was not to be just yet. Indeed what he learned from Tim and Rob, confirming his suspicions of a roughing-up which had gone wrong, did anything but calm his troubled breast.

He had nearly not opened what appeared to be the usual sort of charity begging letter, destining it, rather in the manner of Harry Keene and his Kleenex, for the nearest wastepaper basket, until he noticed that it had been made to look as though it were re-directed to him and that it bore a Grimeford postmark. Tim was obviously trying to be careful. The note inside had said simply "Meet us on Platform 3, Sheffield Midland, 3.00pm, 3rd October".

As Quakke had no lectures to give that afternoon, he was able to get to Sheffield without alerting anyone at the University to anything unusual. Lucy would not expect him home until at least seven as he quite often worked on in his office until late. If there were to be any emergency and she should ring and ask for him, he would have to deal with that problem. Unless he absolutely had to, he wasn't going to get Lucy involved in this at all.

They shook hands as he got off the train. Just two lads meeting their dad, or uncle, maybe. Quakke had thoughtfully put on the flat cap he wore for gardening which he thought might make him appear the average northern man in the street. Tim and Rob were bare-headed, but were wearing quilted anoraks against the blistering wind which ran through the station like the proverbial dose of salts. Rob got them a polystyrene cup of coffee each and they went up to a seat on the end of the platform, as though waiting for a local train.

Quakke sipped his coffee with knitted brow as Tim, in his best English, related the conversation with Harrison, the lorry driver. Like Quakke with regard to Lucy, Tim was operating a need-to-know policy. He had briefed Rob carefully on this. Rob was a good lad, but his mouth, on occasions, tended to move faster than his brain. This was the sort of occasion. Tim had decided to leave out any reference to attempted rape.

'So,' Quakke summed up, pained enough Tim thought, 'Gemma fell out of the 'police' van and into the path of Harrison's lorry. Another 'officer' was following in Gemma's car. She was taken off in the van and transferred to the car after a fake accident had been staged, then the car was set on fire.'

'Looks like it,' said Tim. 'I don't suppose there's any point in going to the police again?' he continued, seeking advice from the older man.

'The real police?' said Quakke. 'From what you tell me, it doesn't seem likely that they would be interested. They think it's all cut and dried. In any case, if we try to get Harrison prosecuted we shall probably alert whoever it is who's paying him the money and blow for ever our chance of finding out who it is.'

'That's what I thought,' said Rob, determined to get a word in somewhere.

'You don't think this lorry business could be another false trail?' said Quakke whose suspicions were now working overtime.

'No,' replied Tim. 'That cu... clown Harrison couldn't lie to save his bloody life, not when 'e's pis... drunk I mean, at any rate. And, we found this, just where he said he run into 'er.' He produced from his pocket a handkerchief in which was wrapped a small but expensive chain and crucifix. 'It was in the gutter, part-covered by leaves. We nearly missed it. She was wearing it in the Club.'

Quakke blanched as he took the chain which had been round his baby's fragile little neck. 'Her mother bought it for her,' was all he could say for the moment. 'But so far,' he continued, as he regained his composure, 'we have gotten no idea of who these officers were?'

'No,' said Tim grimly, 'complete blank except' he added a detail he had not mentioned before 'one had a cockney accent.'

'Redhead or blond?' asked Quakke with a faraway look. It seemed to Tim a fairly useless distinguishing clue at the stage they were at.

'I expect 'e were wearing a 'elmet,' said Rob, trying to be helpful. 'Any road, I don't suppose Harrison would have noticed if 'e'd been wearin' a bra an' tights,' he continued.

'Bloody shut it, will tha!' hissed Tim in his ear. Fortunately, the Professor did not appear to have heard either of the last two exchanges. His eyes were glazed. London, he was thinking, had always been, for him, bad news.

'We'll keep in touch, then,' said Tim, brisk and businesslike.

'Sure, keep in touch, son,' sighed Quakke. 'Hope springs eternal,' he added, without really knowing why. 'By the way, you'd better have this,' he continued, placing the crucifix in Tim's hand and closing it over it. 'Her mother thinks it probably melted in the crash. Better not open old wounds. She doesn't know I'm here, in any case, and she might wonder where I got it if she finds it lying around. Keep in touch.'

Quakke boarded the next train bound for the West Country, changed at Birmingham New Street and was back in the house for half-past six.

'Had a good day, dear?' asked Lucy.

'Interesting, sugar, no more than interesting,' replied Quakke as he put chunks of ice into a large glass.

Part Three

– – –

Chapter One

Autumn was taking its course, as Autumn does. It had been a long way behind the last horse in the St Leger that particular year, but Nature had begun to compensate with rain and violent wind which meant that the deciduous leaves would be fallen before the first snow came, if indeed it did. The miners were equally deciduous. Things had turned out very much as Sir Julian Callendar had predicted, and, of course, engineered. Only a handful of militant colliers were hanging on now, out of pride rather than in expectation of victory, stubbornly refusing to be crushed under the heel of the oppressor, stubbornly, perhaps, failing to admit that when defeat eventually came, it would be their pits which bore the brunt of closures. In that sense, they might have argued, they had nothing to lose. Grimeford lads were among this remnant.

'We shall 'ave to get this sorted before we go back to work,' Tim had said to Quakke.

'Or we might 'ave a lot of time on us 'ands,' Rob had muttered lugubriously.

Time on their hands they did have at the moment, there being no picketing to do and no visible developments on the Gemma front. Rob had been all for going off to London, mostly because, inexplicably in these times of rapid travel and broad interests, he had only been once and that to a rugby league final when he had arrived on a coach and left on the same day, drowning his sorrows some way up the M1. Tim had dissuaded him, however, arguing with some cogency that they would need the money if they ever had a lead to follow up, it being unlikely that looking for somebody in London with a cockney accent, even supposing it was a redheaded man which was the best possible scenario, would bring more than total frustration.

It was thus that they found themselves at the last Flat Race Meeting of the season at Grimeford Racecourse. Miners have traditionally supported racing creatures of all kinds, whether it be horses, dogs, or pigeons, partly out of the freedom that they represent as opposed to the incarceration inherent in spending eight hours or more at a time underground, partly, perhaps, out of the same spirit of gambling which is implied by espousing a dangerous occupation. Not that they had, or would gamble large amounts of money.

'We could do wi a sugar daddy like yon' bastard Harrison,' said Rob, referring to the handouts the ex-lorry driver was apparently still receiving, in spite of his avowed dislike of blood-money. He tore up his betting slip from the first, and in his case unsuccessful, race.

'Wi' thy knowledge of 'orses it ud mek no difference,' replied Tim, thinking about chiding him for the tastelessness of the remark, but deciding, on short odds, against.

'What does tha reckon fer this next un then?' asked Rob. 'Thy turn, all profits shared. What we agreed.'

'Who's more likely to share whose profits?' asked Tim, rhetorically. 'Let's 'ave a look at t' Racing Post.'

A no more than cursory glance told him that in this seven furlong handicap Grimeford Lad was the form horse. 'Top weight an' all. Always go for t' top weight in a 'andicap, I'n't that what they say?'

'That's what tha said last time. It wor a bloody donkey. Came in last.'

'You can never tell wi' 'andicaps,' said Tim, defensively. 'Two quid Tote? Each way?'

'Nay, go fer t' win,' cajoled Rob. 'Muck or nettles.'

As Tim reached into his anorak pocket for the required stake, he came across a piece of paper. As he drew it out he realised it was a betting-slip which bore the legend 'Titanic Struggle – to win, 2.30 Grimeford.'

'How the 'ell did that get there!' he ejaculated.

'Why worry? Finders keepers. Never look a gift 'orse in the mouth,' shrugged Rob who was in proverbial mood. 'Might as well gi' it a go.'

Titanic Struggle came in at ten to one. Rob was jubilant. Tim was still wondering where the bet came from. As he collected the winnings he was looking over his shoulder in case somebody suddenly pounced and claimed them, but nobody did.

'We'll put it towards London,' he said.

'We can 'ave a bevy on the stake, though,' suggested Rob. 'That cost us nowt.'

Tim didn't disagree. Five hundred pounds was a lot of money and he needed a drink to get over the shock. The bar was crowded and it was almost impossible to get served. Tim used some scrum tactics, pushing his way through, wincing slightly as his newly-restored arm felt the brunt of a shoulder charge. He apologised as he bumped into a dark-skinned, good-looking woman who nodded gently in acknowledgement and gave him a smile which sent a shiver down his spine. There was something familiar about her. There had been some famous writer taking an interest in the women's groups, Gemma had told him, but he had never seen her. He would have noticed, he thought, as he jockied further forward. He had always fancied what they called ironically down the pit 'a bit o' black'. He put that out of his mind for the moment, it seeming somehow incongruous with his new role of Knight-Errant or Avenging Angel, and shrugging off a tackle by a weasely-looking youth, he got to the bar. It crossed his mind that he might have had his pocket picked, but he reached into his anorak and brought out what he thought was a tenner. With a mixture of surprise and horror as his heart started to beat again he stared at the betting-slip: 'Cockney Striker: 3.30 – to win.' The stake was again £50. 'Aw, bloody 'ell,' he said to himself, but managed to pick up two double whiskies and get back to where Rob was waiting.

'I know,' he said, hurriedly, before Rob could open his mouth.

'Never look a gift 'orse...'

It seemed like about three hours before the three-thirty was run. Tim tried to calm his nerves by drinking the whisky and looking out for the beautiful dark woman, but he couldn't see her and he assumed some influential acquaintance was entertaining her somewhere. Actually, he wasn't wrong. He was relieved when Cockney Striker came in third by two lengths.

'Oh well, nothing risked, nothing lost,' said Rob cheerfully. It was not a proverb Tim recognised.

They stayed to the end of the meeting, eyed up the horses but didn't have another bet, eyed up the girls, but couldn't find any who were unaccompanied. As they went into the car-park they had to move pretty smartish to avoid a big black Daimler which seemed in a hurry to get out. It had smoked glass and they couldn't tell who was in it.

'Fuckin' rich gits!' swore Rob. Looking at his windscreen as they neared the car, he exclaimed 'What! A bloody parkin' ticket in a car-park.'

'Curiouser and curiouser, said Alice,' breathed Tim as he read the computer-generated note:

'YOU'VE GOT THE MONKEY, NOW GO FOR THE ORGAN-GRINDER. AWAIT FURTHER INSTRUCTIONS.'

'We'd better see Quakke,' said Tim.

'Who's Alice?' asked Rob.

– – –

Quakke was at the stage when what Christian hope he had left was rapidly giving way to its Pagan sister, revenge. He felt unable to pray any more. As he wrote in his diary:

'Zebra'

'I cannot accept any more that my prayers may be answered in a way I don't want. There seems little point in praying for what God wants. If He is so powerful He can do it for Himself. If what has happened to me so far is supposed to be for my own good I am glad God didn't have it in for me.' The professor, nevertheless, if only out of habit, continued his desultory consultations of the Bible. In Corinthians he happened upon the following verse:

"And no marvel: for Satan himself is transformed into an angel of light"

Did that mean that the perpetrators of evil might be those one would least suspect? The great, if not, deep down, the good.

Tim might have been forgiven for believing that there was no need for secrecy any more. Some person unknown clearly was aware of who he was and giving him some help towards finding Gemma's killer. He could easily have dropped Quakke a line telling him about the extraordinary events at the Racecourse and including the typed note. Fortunately, partly because he enjoyed the idea of the cloak if not the dagger, he kept up the disguised letter ploy.

Quakke opened the Greenpeace circular which had been sent onto him from Grimeford and made a mental note to meet the lads at Birmingham New Street the following day.

He heard Tim's story once, then asked for the main details to be repeated. He could leave out the fantasies about coloured girls and how bad the burgers were, thought Quakke.

'The betting-slips were clearly put in your pocket when you were in a crowd – the second one probably when you thought you'd had your pocket picked,' he said.

'Ah'd worked that aht missen,' scoffed Rob, obviously disappointed in the fruits of Academic training. 'It's findin' out who did it that's t' problem.'

'Not necessarily yet,' Tim reminded him – '"Await further instructions". It's who they're leading to we want to find out.'

'Or away from,' mused Quakke, recollecting his Bible text.

'You mean somebody's trying to put us off t' scent?' asked Rob.

'By fingering somebody else?' asked Tim.

'Precisely,' went on Quakke. 'Let's see if the messages themselves give us a clue as to who is being fingered.'

'There was only one message,' said Rob.

'What about the betting-slips?'

'You think the names of the 'orses 'ave something to do wi' it?' asked Tim, catching Quakke's drift.

'Sure,' replied the Professor. 'Only one of them won. That might have been a coincidence. I think it's the names that are important.'

'Right,' said Tim. 'Titanic Struggle. Are they telling us it's somebody to do wi' boats?'

'The...er... Titanic struggle would refer, I think,' replied Quakke, slipping into lecturing mode, 'to the clash of the Titans...'

'Wa'n't that a film?' cut in Rob.

''Appen,' snarled Tim. 'Ler 'im carry on, Rob.'

'The Titans,' continued Quakke, clearing his throat and taking a sip of cold coffee, 'were sons and daughters of Uranus and Ge.'

'Whose anus?' asked Rob.

'Bloody shut it will tha?' said Tim with a laugh.

'Sons and daughters of Uranus and Ge,' harrumphed Quakke. He was grateful he didn't have students like this at the University. 'Uranus had gotten rid of his other children by Ge, sent them to the underworld. The Titans deposed him and liberated their brothers.'

'That's a lot of people,' said Tim. 'What's the idea of the message, then?'

'That we are dealing with somebody important,' said Quakke, ' but then we knew that with all that money flying about.'

'That's still more than one,' objected Tim, 'we are looking for that cockney who was responsible for Gemma's death aren't we? Cockney Striker sounds more like it to me.'

'Ye.. es,' said Quakke thoughtfully, 'but what if whoever it is who's setting somebody up were telling us Cockney Striker wasn't the person ultimately responsible? If I had to pick out one of the Titans, it would have to be Kronos who took Uranus' place as King. And Kronos was a dangerous man. He cut off his father's genitals with a sickle given him by his sister.'

'Nice one,' said Tim, whistling softly.

'We should a' done that ter that bugger Harrison,' put in Rob.

'That doesn't tell us who Kronos is, though,' said Tim. 'What about Cockney Striker? If we were talking about the cockney we're looking for trying to implicate this Kronos, whoever he is, that explains the Titanic Struggle, but he wouldn't be trying to get himself in trouble, would he? He might not even know Harrison's told us anythin' about 'im bein' a cockney. An' what does "Striker" suggest? He wouldn't want to tell us he'd been involved in ought to do wi' t' strike.' He was lapsing into the vernacular as he became excited in the reasoning into which Quakke had led him.

'I'm not sure about that one yet, Tim,' said Quakke, 'although I think you have made two good points which amount to the same damned thing in the end. Cockney Striker is trying to get – Kronos, let's call him, into trouble and Kronos is trying to get Cockney Striker into trouble, we may assume, at the moment, unknown to each other.'

'Oh aye!' said Rob, illuminated.

'It's a good job you're still being careful about communication, Tim,' continued the Professor. 'We don't want them to find out. We'll learn more like that.'

'I suppose one could know the other's after 'm an' be settin' us on 'im in retaliation,' suggested Tim.

'Again, a good point, son,' Quakke congratulated him. 'Which of them knows?'

'I'd put my money on Cockney Striker,' said Tim, as Quakke nodded his approval.

'Tha did,' said Rob, 'well, some'dy else's. It lost.'

'We'll see,' smiled the Professor. 'Now what's the monkey got to do with anything?'

'That's easy,' put in Rob. 'A monkey's five hundred quid. That's what we won.'

'And who knew that?' asked Quakke, proceeding to answer himself. 'The person who wrote the first betting-slip.'

'Cockney Striker,' confirmed Tim.

'Centre forward for Chelsea,' said Rob gleefully.

'Shut it, Rob,' said Tim, not for the first time in their detective career and not realising at the time that there is many a true word...

'In figurative terms,' Quakke summed up, 'Cockney Striker is also the monkey to Kronos, the organ-grinder, which confirms both our theory of who wrote which message and the relationship between the two protagonists.'

'I thought you said he cut 'em off?' asked Rob innocently.

– – –

The train pulled smoothly out of the dark Satanic piles of New Street Station and proceeded northwards. Heading for what he still considered – but only just – the real world, Tim began, for the first time, to have cold feet. It was patently obvious now that he was involved with something big, important people and all that. Could he handle it? When it had first occurred to him to track down Gemma's killer it had been more in the cowboy spirit – perhaps a long horse pursuit, rope the bandit round the feet and drag him off to the Sheriff. Now it appeared that not only was he chasing somebody with a faster horse, but that there were two bandits each trying to use him to bring down the other. Would he get caught in the middle? He was bound to fail in the eyes of one of them. Having done so, would he himself end up the victim of some gruesome 'accident'? Wouldn't he be better to leave it to Quakke? He had the brains after all and he did have some importance. He was a professor. There would be more questions asked about his demise than about Tim's.

The train jolted to a halt, throwing against Tim a steward carrying a pot of coffee. The latter managed to maintain balance, but only by bracing a left arm against Tim. Tim felt a twinge in his shoulder.

'Sorry, mate,' apologised the steward.

'S awright, mate,' said Tim, lost in his thoughts

How had he got into this mess? Gemma. She awakened in him more tender considerations before he continued his ratiocination. His mother had always told him to beware of strange women, but he had always put down this calumny on her own sex to possessive maternal jealousy. Maybe she'd had a point, as had his mates who had warned him not to go playing out of his league. Why did he keep thinking about football? That joke of Rob's about

Cockney Striker, he supposed. He couldn't chicken out now, though. It was not in his character. He couldn't let Gemma down, nor Quakke, of whom he had grown quite fond in an amused sort of way, and Lucy, that poor woman who had already spent most of her best years in prison, lost her daughter, and now didn't even know what was going on on her behalf. Anyway, Rob would probably never speak to him again if he did. The only thing he could do at the moment was wait. For the first time in his life, he prayed. 'O God, please let me sort out this mess. Amen.' He was not sure he had done it properly. Perhaps he would ask Quakke when he saw him next. He looked a religious man.

They got off at Doncaster, where Tim had left his car, being able to drive again now.

At the barrier he fumbled for his ticket.

'That's not a ticket, lad,' said the perplexed ticket-collector who handed back a thin piece of card.

'Sorry,' said Tim, handing over the real ticket.

He paused for a moment in the entrance hall to look at the card.

'Ah don't know,' replied Tim. 'Ah don't know what to mek o' this.'

Written on the card, in block capitals, was the exhortation:

"KEEP 'OPE IN YER 'EART"

'Ah'll gi' it some thought,' said Tim.

– – –

It was a warm night for November. He couldn't sleep. He was thinking about the bit of card first of all. Was it another message from one or other of the Titans? If so, which one? It looked like Cockney – no aitches. It was an instruction of sorts and it was Cockney Striker who had told him to wait for instructions, but it wasn't much use in that direction. It was more the sort of thing Quakke might have said to him. Perhaps Quakke was having a little game with him, poking gentle fun at the same time at his own lack of aspirates. Blank.

Then he was tossing and turning. 'More tossin' than turnin', I bet!' Rob might have said. And he was dreaming. He was in a private box at the Racecourse, making love on golden sheets to a beautiful dark woman with luscious pink lips at both ends. Then he woke up. His dick was sore and he had to go and change his pyjamas and move the sheets around so he didn't sleep in the wet patch. He fell asleep once more, turning, turning, turning, walking down a long, dark corridor which eventually merged into a tall, high-walled toilet with white tiles everywhere and he was stood between two walls having a slash and the walls were closing in and he couldn't move. He was rooted to the spot.

He woke up in a sweat, decided he needed to go to the toilet and reached for the bedside lamp. A fairly substantial newspaper fell to the floor and, as he eventually found the switch to the table-lamp, he found it was the Racing Post he had brought back from the Race Meeting. He took it to the toilet with him. He tried to put the seat down gently, but it fell with a bang on the porcelain. He sat down.

'What are tha laikin' at?' came an angry voice from his parents' bedroom.

'Just going to t' toilet, dad.'

'Well bloody 'urry up. We're trying to get some sleep in 'ere.'

'Right,' Tim muttered.

He looked again at the two races the 'message' horses had been in. He didn't normally bother with the pedigrees, but just marking time while the necessaries took place, he looked at Titanic Struggle. It was by Kronos out of Battle of Britain. Quakke's theory was right then, without a doubt, but who WAS Kronos and did Battle of Britain mean anything?

He flushed the toilet, ignored groans of 'Bloody 'ell!' coming from the parental nest and went back into his own room.

3.30. Cockney Striker. By Old Bill out of Maradonna.

'Fuckin' football,' said Tim out loud with rather more than the rugby-player's frustration at the popularity of the inferior game. Another moan from next door told him it was time for his third attempt to get some decent sleep.

— — —

Fascinated as he was by the exegesis of betting-slips, Quakke had felt just as frustrated as Tim by the discovery that there was a battle of wills going on. If there was one thing he hated more than a learning curve (one of the many modern semantic developments of which he did not approve, but found himself mixed up in all the time) it was a non-learning spiral.

Fortunately, he was able to get rid of his frustration, unlike Tim, without recourse to wet dreams and trips to the toilet. Lucy found him more ready than ever to satisfy both his and her marital needs and she was gratified to see how well Hymer was coping with the bereavement. She was especially happy that he was not diving into conspiracy theory again, it being her abiding belief that it was best to let bygones be has-beens, or vice-versa.

Thus well had the Professor hidden from his wife his real preoccupations and when he received a letter from the Society for the Preservation of Bird-Life in Mongolia and Lucy commented on the amount of junk mail he was receiving lately, he was inclined to put off a response to Tim's request for another pow-wow for at least a week, since it was only two days since he had seen him last and it was his own summing-up of the situation that both parties in the Titanic Struggle would want to play it cagey at this stage, being only willing to let the greyhounds from the slips when they were sure that the quarry could be finished off without being alerted.

The thought of finishing-off worried him for a moment – what were they going to do with either one or both of the two when or if they caught up with them? – but he managed to put it out of his mind, consoled himself with the counter-thought that perhaps things were nearer to a finish than he had imagined and, acting on his own dictum, often expressed to students hoping to hand in essays late, that 'Procrastination ruins your foresight', he invented an emergency meeting of the University Senate and set off for Chesterfield.

– – –

It was not an ideal venue. Railway stations in November, even with an unseasonal burst of warmth, such as Tim was experiencing, are not at their most welcoming. The three of them opted to perambulate rather than to sit freezing in one place and they went down to a nice little park with a cricket field.

'Came 'ere once to a Sunday League match,' said Rob, who was experienced in sporting excursions.

Quakke, who was neither interested in cricket – he couldn't understand it – nor in being brought this distance to indulge in idle chatter, waited until they were out of earshot of all the crumb-hunting birds, then he said, 'This had better be good.'

After a warning to Rob not to 'piss about', Tim outlined what he thought he had now learned.

'You were definitely right, in every detail, about the struggle,' he concluded, 'and we now know for definite Cockney Striker was the man responsible for Gemma's death. Old Bill means he was the bogus policeman. Maradonna suggests that Striker points to football rather than being off work...'

'Ah said that,' put in Rob.

'So tha did,' said Tim, seeing Quakke's impatience and continuing. 'The one thing I can't make any sense of is Battle of Britain. Everything else means something, so that must do an' all.'

'Your logic is commendable, young man,' smiled Quakke. 'All of this arose out of the strike, didn't it? That's the only Battle of Britain which has been going on recently. Cockney is telling us his enemy has something to do with the strike.'

'He's not a miner,' said Rob.

'No, sirree,' said Quakke. 'This is a man with power. The power to break strikes...or make them. Perhaps both. Perhaps his cockney enemy was once his friend, his henchman, perhaps he got things wrong.'

'In that case,' breathed Tim, 'we 'd better be bloody careful.'

'I think that would be wise,' nodded the Professor.

'By the way, that was a bit of a laugh you putting that card in mi pocket,' said Tim. 'You know, when we came to Birmingham. Ah didn't think you 'ad it in yer.'

'Palpably not,' grimaced Quakke. 'I didn't put any card anywhere. What did it say?'

Tim produced the card from his pocket. Quakke was puzzled. 'Looks like a cockney reference,' he said. 'No aitches. Cockney wouldn't be drawing attention to himself, though.'

'Must be Kronos' work, then, but what is he telling us? "'ope in yer 'eart".'

'An' you'll never walk alone, you'll ne.. e.. ver..'

'Stop pissin' abaht, Rob... hang on, though. It's fuckin' football again!'

'Ah told thee, yer twat,' said Rob, proudly.

'Looks as if the reference to football is being strengthened,' said Quakke.

'Yer mean it's a footballer?' asked Rob.

'Someone to do with football, certainly. All the indications we have so far, however, are of somebody pretty high-powered.'

'A manager or a director? Somebody like that?' asked Tim.

'Could be,' concluded Quakke. 'I'll leave you to do some investigation on that. I have to arrive home at the right time from a Senate meeting. Keep in touch and...'

'We know,' cut in Tim. 'Be careful!'

'Exactly,' confirmed Quakke.

'There WAS one other thing I wanted to ask you,' said Tim as they waited on the station for the Professor's train back to Birmingham.

'Be my guest,' said Quakke.

'How do you pray?' said Tim.

– – –

'Come on then, football's thy game,' said Tim to Rob as they sat in their own train travelling towards Sheffield. 'Who are we after?'

'Ah know players, me,' said Rob. 'Ah don't know directors and such like.'

'Tha must read t' gossip in t' papers an' what not. Managers an' so on are 'igh profile nowadays. Owt been goin' on recently?'

'There was that Chesterham chairman what resigned not long sin',' suggested Rob. 'Fritzy Freeman.'

'Go on,' Tim encouraged him.

'It were funny like 'cos they reckoned there were no rows. There were no financial problems. Not till he left any road.'

'And?'

'Not been heard of sin' then.'

'Curiouser and curiouser.'

'Said Alice?' offered Rob. 'Couldn't be 'im passin' messages, could it?'

'You don't 'ave to be 'ere to pass messages,' said Tim. 'Organ grinders have monkeys.'

'Well, in any case, gerrin' mixed up in this sort o' thing...'

'You heard Quakke. He thinks it's somebody big. Why not t' biggest?'

'If tha puts it like that.'

'Ah do,' said Tim. 'Looks like we'll have to start spendin' some o' that money.'

'It were 'is money, wa'n't it?' said Rob, who had just about followed the plot.

'If it wor 'im, definitely – paid to keep us off 'is track. One of life's little ironies, as they say. We'll drop a note to Quakke, careful, like.'

– – –

By the time Lucy, with raised eyebrows, handed the Professor the circular marked 'Rest Homes for Penguins', the doughty duo were already on their way to London by High Speed Train.

'I'll throw it in the trash bin on my way out, honey,' said Quakke.

'Been getting rather a lot of them recently,' complained Lucy. 'Unsolicited mail. The Government should do something about it.'

In general Quakke was in complete agreement. However, it was serving its purpose at the moment.

After kissing Lucy goodbye, he closed the back door, rattled the dustbin and went down the drive to the car. He drove a couple of miles and pulled up in a shady spot under some nearly naked sycamores. He tore open the envelope and read:

'After prize pig. Capital work. T/R.'

Tim's code was not quite as subtle as the Titans', but he gathered they were following up a lead on Cockney Striker.

'I sure hope those guys are being careful,' he muttered to himself as he moved off towards Lanchester.

— — —

The guys had decided to go to London by train and take a suburban line to Chesterham. Nestling in the stockbroker belt, the town was not one which might traditionally be associated with Association Football, but Freeman, with whose football activities the reader is familiar, had got together a good team. At a time when foreign players were somewhat of a rarity, he had managed to get work permits for a number of European and South American maestros who made up the majority of the first team. Other clubs had complained but it had appeared to make no difference. Not only had Fritzy Freeman had the money to buy players, he had also, it seemed, had influence in the right places. Chesterham United was now one of the top clubs in the First Division and had had a good run in all knockout competitions in the previous season. Money, mostly Freeman's, had also built up impressive sport and leisure complexes around the ground and refurbished the whole stadium. It was a model of sporting enterprise.

Tim and Rob were not expecting to come across Freeman on this visit, but were 'sussing it aht', as Rob put it. It being before noon there was a selection of players' and coaches' vehicles in the official car park, together with the cars of those members of the administrative staff who were charged with the day to day running of the club.

Tim and Rob stood looking at the vast complex and wondering what to do next. Rob, who had been there on one of his excursions with Leeds United was explaining to Tim that the Chesterham mob thought they were "ard cunts', but, he was adding, 'not as 'ard as us'.

A short swarthy man with curly black hair came out to get into the Jaguar parked next to the office block, spotted them and came over. 'Sorry no unauthorised persons on this area,' he said, trying the soft approach first to save himself having to call up Security. (Where were those bastards anyway?) His identity badge proclaimed him Max Greenbaum, Director.

'We were only looking,' said Tim. 'We foller Chesterham, like, and we don't get up to London much. We're interested, like. You don't see much when you come to a match. Mr Freeman did a good job, didn't he?'

'Freeman? What do you know about Freeman?' asked Greenbaum, reaching in his pocket for the phone. 'Not Press, are you?'

'No,' said Tim, 'we...'

'No, you don't look like Press,' Greenbaum assured himself. 'Not some of his mates come to duff me up are yer?' he asked again, suspicious. 'No, you'd have done it by now, that sort. Just clear off then, before I ring for Security.' He started pushing them towards the main gate, then wondering whether he had bitten off more than he could chew, he stopped short again.

'Not filth are yer? Nah, too young for Fraud Squad.'

'We're not really interested in Freeman,' said Rob. Sometimes, thought Tim, this lad is an undiscovered genius.

'Oh!' said Greenbaum, taken by surprise.

'Ah suppose he were a big mate of yours,' continued Rob. Go on, thought Tim to himself, go on.

'I thought he was, before this last business. Then he just upped and left me in the lurch, took out all his capital and left me with best part of three million to find just to keep things going on the football front, not to mention all the other stuff. There's nothing wrong with any of it – perfectly good investment – but when somebody takes off like that everybody else wonders what's round the corner.'

'No word of explanation,' asked Rob.

'Not a dicky. Money's in Switzerland, shouldn't wonder. Bloody Freeman's in the Caribbean. Here, what am I telling you all this for anyway?' said Greenbaum, remembering why he had come over to the lads in the first place.

'Shoulder to cry on?' suggested Tim. Better Rob's than his, though, with his collar bone.

'Clear off now,' urged Greenbaum. 'If Freeman had still been Chairman of this club, you wouldn't have dared set foot anywhere you weren't authorised.'

'Violent man, is he?' asked Tim innocently.

'You could say that,' shuddered Greenbaum as Tim and Rob left the premises, saying a small thanksgiving to Jehovah that these weren't friends of Fritzy's.

– – –

'Shall we carry on where we left off in that suite at Grimeford Racecourse?' suggested Kronos. 'It was a lovely atmosphere with the flowers, the gold silk sheets and you, bien sûr.' He opened Kaki's mouth gently and slid his tongue around her teeth. 'You were so good too at slipping that boy our note I didn't realise that you were so accomplished at leger-de-main.'

'And Birmingham? Don't forget Birmingham,' Kaki scolded him.

'And Birmingham,' Kronos cooed. 'How could I forget Birmingham? Dreadful, common place. Took my chauffeur an hour to get out of the bloody place. But you're right, you were bloody marvellous as a Jamaican tea-lady.'

'Coffee-lady,' Kaki corrected him.

'Can one say 'coffee-lady'?' asked Kronos, getting precious. 'I suppose one will one day, the state of the English language being what it is. I suppose a liberationist like yourself should actually designate it coffee-person. It just sounds so vulgar. Just like dear old Brum.'

They both laughed.

'They're on to him now, I'm delighted to tell you. They've paid a visit to Chesterham, according to my little girl who works in the office and had a word with good old garrulous Max.'

'What do you mean 'your little girl'?' teased Kaki, unbuttoning his shirt. 'I'm your little girl, aren't I?'

'You're my BIG girl,' said Kronos, 'I'm glad to say.'

Kaki giggled as she undid the belt of his trousers.

'So, are we having the Champagne now?' she wheedled.

'I think, on mature reflexion, we'll take a rain check on it, or whatever those dreadful yanks say. I'll make do with this,' he said slipping the skimpy white dress down over her firm body and pulling her to him.

'Does that mean the Champagne's a bigger treat than I am?' pouted Kaki.

'It means, darling,' said Kronos, snuggling down into the crinkly, black hair, 'that I can wait for the Champagne.'

Chapter Two

Hymer had now only one obsession – vengeance. Calvinist by upbringing, he was rapidly being converted to Jesuitic tendencies. When Tim had asked him about praying, he had been careful to tell him to conclude his intercessions with 'thy will be done', but since he was unclear what God's will would be in the present matter and not at all anxious for some act of providence to protect Gemma's killer (whom he was now nearly certain they had found) from his just deserts, he preferred to exercise his own will. Any sin he might commit in the course of this exercise would be excused by the purity of its intention.

With this preoccupation and an ever increasing worry that, if things hotted up, Lucy might become suspicious, he had abandoned all thoughts of self-improvement. He had taken up smoking again – Thank God (Whoops! Hint of Providence there!) Lucy thought the pipe distinguished – and he was drinking a little bit more, but the irritating personality traits had not come back and he never had nightmares about Nathalie Weinburger these days. The diary had gone, too.

'Friday 18th November 1984'

'I am making this my last entry in this journal. It is perhaps just another habit, after all. If the worst comes to the worst and I am not able – ever – to record my thoughts again, I hope that, at least, my earlier entries will stand as a testimony to my efforts to be a 'good' man.'

As he lay in bed the next morning, Quakke heard the snap of the letter-box. Having no lectures that morning, he was tempted to turn over and go back to sleep, especially since Lucy had not stirred again after getting up at three o'clock to make a cup of tea and have a little weep, which she did sometimes when her courage ran out, but he was concerned that the Yorkshire guys' trip to London might bring another message and he didn't want Lucy to find it. He picked up the envelope bearing the legend 'Aardwark Rescue', tore it open feverishly and read

'Just five pounds of your money could save three of these beautiful animals from extinction...'

Gratefully, he tore the circular to shreds and, putting them in the pedal-bin, went back to bed.

Lucy, wearily half-opening her eyes, asked:

'Was there any post?'

'Aardwaarks,' grunted Hymer.

'Well, I only asked,' said Lucy.

When they finally got up about eleven, Quakke fixed brunch, as he called it. Relief at not being called out had given him an appetite, although a concern did linger at the back of his mind. He squeezed fresh orange juice, fried bacon, eggs and fillet steak, and knocked up pancakes with maple syrup.. Lucy managed a bit of toast and two boiled eggs.

'Fancy going out?' asked Quakke. 'It's a nice bright day.'

'Why not?' said Lucy.

They put on walking-boots and strolled along the river bank. They sat on the bridge at Downton, throwing bits of twig into the fast-flowing water.

'Wouldn't it be lovely if we could put all our troubles on those little boats and let them float away out of reach for ever?' suggested Lucy. 'Totally destroy anything but the present.'

'Look, mine's gotten stuck on that weed over there,' said Quakke. They crossed the bridge and went up the other side of the river.

'You're quiet,' said Lucy.

'Just admiring the scenery,' lied Hymer. Shouldn't I give up this lark? he was thinking. For Lucy's sake. It's getting harder and harder to conceal it. Then – No, I'm doing it for Lucy's sake – No, you're not, said the first voice inside him, it's for your own stupid pride. For Gemma – Fat lot of use to her. Well, decency, justice... Get yourself killed for an abstract? taunted the other voice. The guys, all the trouble they're going to – They're young, they'll get over it. If I don't go through with this I shall never forgive myself, said the first voice and this time there was no answer.

'Did I tell you there was a conference coming up in London?' he asked.

'No,' said Lucy. 'When?'

'I've left the details at the faculty,' said Quakke. Lucy knew he could be forgetful. 'I'll pick 'em up later and let you know. He was preparing her for the time when he was convinced he would have to take a more active, perhaps even decisive, part in the battle of the Titans.

They went on in silence, shovelling through the damp red, brown and orange leaves on the path. They held hands. From time to time they kissed. To the rare observer just a happy couple on a weekend walk.

– – –

The reader may now be wondering what Freeman aka Logos, the second person in the unholy trinity, was up to during this time. His messages passed on to Tim in more or less the same manner as Kronos – no surprise really when people have worked together – were evidence of his plan, his control – his supposed control, that is. Having spent a couple of days stashing his assets in Zurich, Freeman was enjoying his stay in the Antilles, doing the things he liked most – screwing beautiful women and hurting people. The former were no trouble. Money is a powerful aphrodisiac and Fritzy was not short of that. It readily compensated for his pendulous stomach and his balding pate, not to mention his false teeth, most of the real ones having been extracted by worthy opponents in those struggles we have recorded earlier. The latter involved a little more effort. It involved going round the bars, picking some bloke who was drunk enough to fight, but not sober enough to win, giving him a good kicking, slashing his face with a Stanley knife or glassing him in the time-honoured manner. The police didn't seem to worry. If they did think of these incidents as anything more than the concomitants of tourist enjoyment, they would hardly be coming looking for a fat-cat philanderer slumped next to his latest conquest by the pool of the best hotel in town. No. He was safe, he was enjoying himself and he was pleased both with the messages he had put in Tim's way and with the fact that, for once, he was up on Kronos. He knew Kronos was out to get him, but Kronos didn't know what he knew and soon those lads and that nutty professor would be on his tail. He would soon be going back to London to see to that himself. It was known in his trade as getting your retaliation in first.

If Logos had listened to Sir Hugh Carvem-Downe more intently on those occasions he had sat drinking brandy with him in the Antidiluvian Club, he might have learned that the indispensable tactic involved in both attack and defence is to cover your rear. We can imagine what raucous rejoinder he might have added to that remark. However, he had probably been muttering 'Stupid old git' or something of that ilk, and continued dreaming of his next punch-up. If he had listened, he would have taken more care to keep an eye out for happenings at Chesterham United. He might then have known that Tim and Rob were on his trail rather than Kronos'. The Logos we know never looked back.

'Get us another drink, dahlin',' said Sir Fritz, slapping hard on the skimpily clad buttocks of the tall blonde girl who was lying face down next to him.

'Ouch! That hurt,' said the girl, too aware of Logos' propensities to disobey, and scrambling off towards a trolley parked at the challenging distance of five yards. They were in a private little pool-side venue where anything could, and usually did, happen.

Karen came back with the double gin and tonic and a Bacardi and coke for herself. When he was in this mood, it was well to think about anaesthesia.

'To crime,' said Logos, clinking glasses, 'to sweet, sweet revenge'. Karen didn't know what he was talking about and thought it better not to ask. Perhaps she could wheedle him back into one of his better moods.

'Fritzy,' she cajoled, stroking the hairs on his chest. 'Couldn't we go out? Down the coast or somewhere?'

'What do we want to go out for?' replied Freeman. 'When we've got everyfing vat's necessary here?'

Karen's anaesthesia went flying as Fritzy turned her over on her front once more, tore off her bikini bottom, parted her legs and entered her from behind.

Chapter Three

Kaki was to take part in a discussion on the role of the working mother in modern society. She was totally focussed, as she left the flat in Knightsbridge she had been sharing with Kronos, on what she was going to say. She hardly noticed that she got into an ordinary black London cab and gave the driver his instructions. She took out a notepad from her handbag and began marshalling a few last minute ideas. It was not until, anxious about the time, she cast a glance at her watch and then out of the window, that she realised she was not heading for the television studios after all, but out of town.

'Hey, stop! This is the wrong way. Turn round,' she shouted at the driver, frantically banging on the glass separating panel.

'Oh no it's not dahlin',' replied a voice she knew all too well. 'An' you're locked in. This is where Mr Big Boots starts to get his comeuppance.'

No use struggling, thought Kaki to herself. Julian will get me out of this. If this fool lays a hand on me, he must know he's dead meat.

'What's it feel like bein' bait?' laughed Freeman as he pulled on to the M4. He was feeling particularly happy since he had managed a nice little literary tour de force which would point the hounds in the right direction – to Kaki and thence to Kronos.

– – –

News of the disappearance of writer, feminist lecturer and TV personality Julie Kerry completed the cast list for Quakke, even before he read the message that Tim had sent him summoning him to the capital. Fortunately, he thought as he got off the train at Euston, he had already given himself an excuse to go up to London, and equally fortunately he had been spot-on with the timing. He had booked himself, Tim and Rob into an hotel in Russell Square which he had used before when going to conferences. Julie, the friend of Julian. It all began to fit into place now. Kerry – Ker, the angel of death. It WAS those three who had caused the trouble in Tolbridge. Now Cockney Striker was telling them for definite who Kronos was – Sir Julian Callendar, Permanent

Secretary to the Home Office and friend, supposedly, of Lucy. Oh God! Lucy!

He tried to phone her, but no one answered. She had had an invitation to stay with some friends in Banbury, he remembered. He hadn't bothered to ask which friends – he had been so wrapped up in the Titanic affair. Supposing... She would certainly ring him that evening. She had his number at the hotel. All he could do was hope and... pray – strange things he had not done for what seemed a long time.

Tim had brought the car down this time and they picked him up. To polite enquiry about his health, he had to respond that he didn't feel too good. Apart from the gastric upset that this business was causing him, he had been unable to sleep the night before until the fourth double whisky and he was feeling the effects, even in the following afternoon.

'You don't need a doctor, do you?' asked Tim, concerned at Quakke's appearance.

'No, no, I think I shall be alright,' said Quakke, for his own as well as the guys' benefit.

'My auntie never went to a doctor in 'er life,' volunteered Rob. 'Not even when she had cancer.'

'And was she OK?' asked Hymer solicitously.

'No, she died,' said Rob.

It broke the tension somewhat. Quakke tried to laugh, even though it reminded him of his headache.

They drove to the hotel and after various ablutions met in the bar for a drink. Quakke had a double Alka-Seltzer.

'We can't talk about what you know here,' said Tim. 'Let's go up to our room.' He and Rob were sharing.

'What if it's bugged?' offered Rob.

'Good point, Rob,' said Tim. Rob seemed pleased his contributions were now being appreciated. Quakke thought it unlikely. On the other hand, if Kronos now knew that Cockney Striker was trying to use them to punish him... and if Cockney Striker was keeping tabs on their progress...

'We'll take a tour round the block,' he said. He thought it might help to clear his head.

Tim showed him the latest piece of the jigsaw:

"FIND THE LADY..."

Quakke slipped into lecture mode again.

'Clearly a reference to Miss Kerry.' He explained the dual nature of her name and how she fitted into the picture.

'She is the picture,' said Rob. 'It's a card game.'

'Precisely,' said Quakke. 'Three cards – Three Titans, an unholy trinity. Let's call the second one Logos.'

'Or Freeman,' said Tim.

'More than likely,' said Quakke. 'Let's continue:'

> "Where the flower goes straight,
>
> Think of two or four or eight.
>
> Find a house without foundation,
>
> Colours of the British nation."

'That's got me flummoxed,' said Tim. 'what have flowers got to do wi' it. Where 'as 'e tekken 'er?'

'Perhaps it's not flower, but flow-er,' suggested Quakke, who had been known to do the odd crossword, especially during senate meetings. 'Something which flows.'

'Like a river, you mean?' asked Rob. It was not his most outrageous piece of speculation.

'Exactly,' said Quakke, 'but which river?'

'Could be the Thames,' said Tim.

'It's a long river, though. Let's see if anything else in this dreadful doggerel can help us. "Where the flower goes straight." We're looking for a straight bit. Not many on the Thames I shouldn't think, not long stretches anyway.'

'Think of two or four or eight,' continued Quakke. 'Two, four, or eight what?'

'Happens at those times?' said Tim.

'Could be,' said Quakke. 'can you think of anything that happens on a river at those times?'

'Tides?' suggested Rob.

'Ingenious,' Quakke congratulated him. 'Can you have three tides? Must be something simpler. Cockney Striker... er Logos isn't that clever or he wouldn't have gotten himself into this mess. Must be something on the river.'

'Boats?' said Rob.

'Trust thee to come up with the bloody obvious...' said Tim.

'That's what we want,' said the Professor, 'something bloody obvious. Boats, not two, four or eight boats, though, surely?'

'Oars,' said Rob.

'Ah beg thi pardon,' said Tim.

'Oars,' repeated Rob, 'number in a boat.'

'Magnificent, young Rob,' said Quakke. Boating. We need a long straight stretch of river good for boating, competitive boating by the sound of it.'

'London?' suggested Rob, who had never had an excursion to the Boat Race, but had heard of it.

His batteries were perhaps running out, Tim thought.

'I don't think so,' said Quakke gently. 'Long and straight. What's that place they have races?'

'Oh, what do they call it? a Regatta.'

'That's it!' said Quakke. 'Henley Regatta. The lady's in Henley.'

'What do these other bits mean then?' asked Tim.

'I think we could leave those till we get there,' said Quakke. 'They might make more sense in situ.'

'Wheer?' said Rob.

'Shut it, yer daft twat,' said Tim, relieved his mate was back to normal.

There was no point in setting off for Henley that night. Logos would not be hanging around and they would have trouble finding their way round an unfamiliar town at night. If Kronos did know they were involved, he would be on their tail, Quakke reasoned. He must see if Lucy was alright. Again no answer. They had dinner. At nine o'clock having tried several times he was hoping for a call from Lucy.

'It's alright, darling,' she said, when to his great relief he heard her voice. 'I'm at Annie's in Banbury. Julian's here, terribly upset about Julie. No news about her, yet. Julian thinks she might have been kidnapped.'

'And I bet he's a good idea who by,' said Quakke softly.

'What's that dear?' said Lucy.

'I said "Nice of him to drop by",' lied Hymer.

'Sleep tight, then, darling. Have a good conference tomorrow,' said Lucy noisily blowing him kisses.

In actual fact Quakke was destined to have neither.

– – –

'I'm getting old,' complained the Dowager Countess Crosse. 'I can't get the spirits down me any more and I have difficulty keeping any other fluids in.' She crumbled a piece of dry toast. 'It is of very little consolation to me that I have a portrait in the attic which looks as young as ever. These are dreadful times. One can't get the servants one used to and the young are so... graceless, present company excepted, of course.'

'Nonsense, auntie,' scolded the tall dark man who made one of the present company, as he helped himself from the array of silver trays on the mahogany sideboard which contained a selection of comestibles from bacon, eggs, kidneys and sausages to kippers and kedgeree. 'Nonsense, I've never known you look so well. You managed that walk around the grounds last evening. Must have been all of three miles.' Julian called the lady "auntie" although she was in fact no blood relation at all, but he had always been able to ingratiate himself into almost any society.

'Not SO long ago,' continued the mistress of Softwicke Hall and Gemma's godmother, 'I could get around the whole estate on horseback. Still I'm not sure I want to go far now with all these dreadful things going on. Permissive Society, I think they call it. In my day...'

'That was twenty years ago, Annie,' laughed Lucy, who, as we have observed, bore no grudges.

'I do hope they find your... er... friend,' rambled the Countess eyeing "The Oxford Mail" over the top of her pince-nez. It would be simply too awful after that accident of poor Gemma's.' She held out a consoling hand towards Lucy, who tried a faint smile of gratitude.

'You mean two looks like carelessness,' grunted Julian through a mouthful of scrambled egg.

'You do say some terrible things sometimes, Julian dear, still, I expect you're upset. Not a lead in sight according to the paper.'

'Do you think there'll be a ransom demand?' asked Lucy.

'I don't know for sure,' replied Callendar, 'but as these things go, I should have received it by now. Unfortunately, that would appear to be the best scenario. The others are that Julie has taken off of her own accord, that somebody is holding her to punish me, or that the same somebody has killed her for the same reason.'

'And you think you know who that somebody is?' asked Lucy.

'I think I do,' said Callendar.

'Terrible times,' said the Countess, shaking her head. 'Terrible, terrible times!'

– – –

'Ah'll have yours if yer don't want it,' said Rob, his mouth already full of sausage and indicating the full English Breakfast which Quakke had pushed away from him.

'Don't be bloody ignorant. This is a posh 'otel,' whispered Tim, casting a glance round the other fast-breakers.

'Why, what's the odds?' protested Rob, sliding unceremoniously the contents of the Professor's plate onto his own.

'It doesn't matter. Carry on,' urged Quakke with a sip of the black coffee which was the only breakfast he could manage. 'Let the boy have it if he wants. He's going to need his strength more than likely.' He toyed with the permutations of the condemned man eating a hearty breakfast, then, confident, with the lack of developments in the last eighteen hours or so, that nobody, at any rate, was bugging them, he said:

'Just carry on eating. I'll sum up what I think the situation is.' Indistinguishable grunts and chompings, interspersed with slurps of coffee.

'Logos...'

'That's Cockney Striker?' Rob wanted clarification.

'Exactly so,' continued Quakke. 'Logos has kidnapped Ker, Julie, whatever you want to call her so that we can find her and from her, find out who Kronos is.'

'But we know already,' spluttered Tim, a toast crumb tickling his throat.

'Yes, but he doesn't know that,' went on Quakke.

'What does he expect us to do, then?' asked Tim, 'torture her until she reveals the dreadful secret?' An unworthy thought prompted by the smile of the dark woman at the races flitted through his mind. He dispersed it with a stab at a nice pink piece of bacon.

'Possibly,' continued Quakke. 'That's the sort of thing he'd do, assuming we are right about his sadistic tendencies. More likely he would expect us to let her go in the hope that sooner or later she would lead us to Kronos.'

'But she'd know we were after Kronos,' put in Tim.

'I guess so,' said Quakke. 'We'd have to be prepared for a showdown with him straightaway if we let her go. Meanwhile, Logos would be nicely out of the way.'

'He could be already,' said Rob, his grey matter fortified by double helpings. 'What has he got to hang about for?'

'My guess is that Logos didn't know that Kronos was after him, yet. He was...'

'Gettin' 'is retaliation in fust,' crunched Rob through a mouthful of toast and marmalade.

'Just as you say,' approved the Professor.

'So, he doesn't know we've been set on to HIM?' confirmed Tim.

'And he will stay around at least long enough to make sure we're on the trail to Kronos.'

'What about Kronos then?' asked Tim. 'What does he know? Does he know what we know?'

'Gets more like Laurel an' 'Ardy 'v'ry minute,' slurped Rob.

Quakke ignored the remark, preferring to concentrate on the synopsis.

'By some miracle Kronos does not yet know Logos has been using us, but he must know by now who is responsible for kidnapping Julie. I think he will have forgotten about us and be in favour of using somebody more professional.'

'More bogus policemen?' queried Tim.

'Or real ones,' said Quakke. 'A crime has been committed and an influential Civil Servant in the Home Office is concerned. Things could get heavy.'

'It's go for the big one first, then,' said Tim.

'I guess so,' sighed Quakke, who was still anxious about Lucy.

'When the goin' gets 'eavy, the 'eavy get goin,' said Rob, sliding in another piece of toast.

'Let's get goin',' agreed Tim. 'Any more toast an' tha'll not get off that Biffo.

'What?' gulped Rob.

'Biffo the Bear – chair – Cockney rhyming slang,' said Tim.

– – –

Logos was worried. It was unlike him, but it was two days now that he had had Julie tied up on the houseboat a business connection had 'lent' him for three grand – no questions asked. It wasn't that he was afraid Kronos – or the police who must be on his tail now – would find him. Fat chance of that. Kronos didn't know he had a boat. He wouldn't think of associating him with Quakke and the miners. With what he'd done to them they were the last people Kronos would expect him to be in contact with. Where were those fuckers by the way? They couldn't be that stupid could they? In another couple of days he might have to get some food in, maybe think of moving Kaki to another hiding-place just to be sure. Why didn't he just cut his losses, kill Julie and clear off to South America? That would really hurt Kronos. He might never get over it. Nah, too easy. Like all rebels, once he had started he wanted to take everything back. He wanted Kronos to be humiliated, to realise he had been outwitted by a superior brain. He would give it two more days, in the meantime sending another literary masterpiece, trying to make it a bit more clear in case those northerners and the American really were a bit dumb for the moment.

'Flowers for me?' said Quakke to an equally surprised receptionist as he was handed the bouquet on his way out to join Rob and Tim in the car. It distracted his mind temporarily from the dilemma: if he didn't tell the guys about the bulge in his pocket (which did not betoken excitement) would they be willing to accompany him to a face-out with Kronos? if he did tell them, would they decide to have nothing to do with it anyway? He took the message and told the receptionist to put the flowers in water.

'They'll do for my funeral,' she thought she heard him say. Flowers again, thought Quakke as he got into the car, and then out aloud to the lads:

'Another summons from Logos. He's getting mighty impatient.'

He read it to them:

"THIS 'ERE RIME IS NOT ERRATIC,

THE BOAT YOU SEEK IS OLD AND STATIC,

PAINTED RED AND BLUE AND WHITE,

ACROSS THE BRIDGE, THIRD FROM THE RIGHT."

'That simplifies things – when we're ready,' said Quakke.

– – –

Kronos, too, was growing anxious. He had heard nothing from Logos. The police had not come up with anything either. Logos had not shown up in any of his usual haunts. Searches at all the properties he owned from warehouses to Breweries, from clip-joints to strip-joints, from hovels to brothels, had all drawn a blank. Logos had not been seen at ports, railway stations, airports or even helicopter pads, but then, if there was one thing he was really good at, it was disguise. If he hadn't left the country, it might mean, at least, that Kaki was still alive. If he had killed her, he kept telling himself – anything to keep up hope – the body would have been found by now and he would have received a gloating message from some gunboat Republic. If Logos was still in England it was because he wanted something other than to hurt Kronos. He wanted to see him hurt. That gave him or the police an outside chance, thought Kronos. Pity those lads hadn't caught up with Logos before he'd started this nonsense, but there was no way Logos was going to get the better of him. Using personality flaws was his speciality.

Chapter Four

A quadrant of the moon was shining eerily over the rooftops still moist from a November frost. In the other direction the sun shone bright and low so that Tim had difficulty driving, the more so since he was not used to getting about London and was trying to concentrate, making sure he didn't unwittingly end up going in the wrong direction down a one-way street. They eventually got out of Russell Square in spite of the rush hour traffic and headed for Whitehall.

'We're not going to the Home Office,' protested Tim. 'We'd never get in there.'

'No,' said Quakke. 'There's a little terrace off the Strand, near Charing Cross Station.' The professor's other precaution, beside the Colt 45, practically unused, which had been handed down to him through two generations of Quakkes, had been to look up in Who's Who, which was a thoughtful addition to the books in the hotel lounge, Sir Julian Callendar. Among other less useful information he had found that Sir Julian belonged to the Antidiluvian Club. Quakke did not know for certain that Sir Julian would be there – after all he had been in Banbury the previous evening – but he guessed that he would be back in London in case of any development on the kidnapping front.

By one of those miracles which occasionally befall the innocent, they managed to park the car near the Station and walked up to the Antidiluvian Club. Quakke was fiddling in his right hand pocket but his hand was shaky and sweaty and rather than risk shooting his foot off, he decided to occupy the hand with his pipe which he withdrew from the other pocket of his jacket and he held it and sucked it at the same time, feeling too sick to light it. What the hell was he doing with a gun anyway? he thought. He didn't even know if it worked and, if it did, what match would he be for somebody who was high up in some kind of secret service – he didn't know which – and was probably a trained killer as well as an habitual manipulator? Was there a gene in his make-up which made him think: trouble – gun?

There was no sign of Callendar's Daimler. It could have dropped him off, of course. He might have gone down to the Home Office. They might as well try again later. They didn't particularly want to attract the attention of the uniformed Commissionaire at the door of the Antidiluvian Club. They walked back up to Trafalgar Square which had not particularly happy memories for Quakke, went right round and headed for the river. They walked the Victoria Embankment, took a quick look at Westminster Abbey, then walked back up Whitehall. Tim and Rob thought Downing Street, at which they cast a quick glance, 'a bit pokey'. They came back, eventually, to the Antidiluvian Club. Another miracle? The black Daimler JC 1 was parked outside.

'Problem number one,' said Rob. 'How do we get in?'

'We'll go round the back,' said Tim, 'an' see if there's a way there.' He felt uneasy himself now. For some reason, the tactics relating to what they were going to do with Kronos when they confronted him did not appear to have been discussed. There were probably enough people in the Club who could see them off, not to mention the police with whom he was so well in. Even if that didn't happen, and they could manage to corner Kronos, what would they do? Beat him up? Revenge would be swift and terrible. Hand him over to the police? On what grounds? Shoot him? Even if they'd had a gun, that didn't seem like a particularly good idea. He only hoped Quakke knew what he was doing.

Round the back of the Club was a courtyard where deliveries were made and rubbish collected. The back of the Club, in contrast to the splendid neo-Elizabethan façade (Quakke's assessment) was what Tim and Rob might have described as grotty. It was in faded red brick and had a fire-escape running up to all four floors.

'We'll get in one o' them fire-doors. They never shut properly,' said Rob who, we remember, was something of an expert in safety. They made their way through the stacks of boxes and crates, some clearly containing the husks of Premier Cru Burgundies and vintage clarets.

'Looks like somebody's had a party,' joked Tim, trying to hide his unease.

'Conservative Party by t' looks on it,' said Rob.

'Shut it, both of you,' hissed Quakke, who was learning fast.

The fire-door on the second floor yielded to a fairly gentle shoulder charge from Tim and they found themselves in a claret-carpeted corridor with embossed Victorian wallpaper in a complementary hue. It led to a sort of antechamber with red velvet sofas and mahogany coffee tables. As they reached it, they looked around carefully, wondering where to go next.

A white-coated steward came out of one of the doors on the left of the antechamber.

''Ere what's goin' on?' he ejaculated. 'Who the hell are you?'

They were about to beat the hastiest of retreats when a voice behind them, well known to Quakke, said:

'It's alright, Peter, I think these gentlemen are looking for me.'

In a flash, the double game had become clear to his acute intellect.

He ushered them up an adjacent staircase to what was obviously a billiard room with a curtained window overlooking the rear courtyard. Tim and Rob who were quite keen on snooker admired to each other the beautifully kept tables.

'So,' said Kronos, sitting on the end of one of them, 'the game is up. I am at your mercy.' He only said that, thought Quakke, because he didn't think it was true. It put him on his guard. His hand moved involuntarily to his right-hand pocket. Kronos did not appear to be alarmed in any way at this movement. Kronos' brain was moving fast. He had forgotten for the moment about these country bumpkins who were to get that common rat, Logos, for him. Now he realised that Logos had been cleverer than he'd given him credit for. These were his hounds as well and, if so, they might lead him to Logos, and, incidentally, to Kaki.

'I think it's Mr Freeman you really want,' he began, trying to lead them in the right direction.

'AND you,' said Quakke, irritated by this man's total gall. 'Remember Ernest Mann and Irma.'

'Suicide on the one hand, a tragic mishap on the other.' Kronos shrugged his shoulders. 'Absolutely no evidence at all which could implicate me. I was sorry about dear Lucy, though, thought she'd get off lightly. She looks very well, by the way, only saw her this morning.'

The mention of Lucy alarmed Quakke. It sounded like a threat. He responded with attack.

'It was you, though, you were behind it, you and your darned Trinity.'

'Well, entre nous, dear boy, continued Kronos, 'we didn't really do much harm. Just removed people we thought could be dispensed with. Mrs Mann got rid of that pompous old fart and you got rid of that old tart of yours and picked up Lucy – eventually', he added ruefully. 'She was liberated from old Lastick and everybody was living happily ever after.'

'Why did you do it?' spluttered Quakke. 'You thought you were God, didn't you?'

'A bit strong, old boy,' said Kronos calmly. 'We were young. It was exciting.'

'But you're still doing it,' objected Quakke.

'If you are referring to the strike,' said Kronos, 'it is true I have played some small part in it, but all in the course of duty. I am simply serving my country. Surely an intelligent man like you can't think that these... goons' he was gesturing towards Tim and Rob. Rob had picked up a billiard cue and was advancing. Tim restrained him.

'Ah should watch it,' he said. ''E's had a 'eavy breakfast.'

'These goons,' the Professor intoned, 'ARE the country. People like you...'

'You are entitled to your opinion,' said the guardian of democracy. 'As I was saying, everybody was living happily until this last and truly lamentable incident. You can't possibly think I had anything to do with that, can you? I can't understand why you are pursuing me.'

'Conscience,' burbled Quakke, worried about what might happen in his right-hand pocket, 'justice...'

'Dearie me,' tutted Kronos. 'We can't live by principles, you know. Those are for the proletariat. To keep them in line.'

'You didn't keep that rotweiler of yours in line did you?'

'Ah, I see,' said Kronos, 'ultimate responsibility. Well, I must admit you have a point there and together I think we ought to make sure that Mr Freeman doesn't get up to mischief again, if you catch my drift.'

'Work with you!' said Quakke, exasperated. Somehow his right hand had left his pocket and a heavy object was wobbling in it. Kronos had just time to duck down behind the table as the lights over the table exploded and Quakke fell over onto Tim and Rob. There was a lot of scuffling and when Tim bundled to the window and drew the curtains there was nothing to be seen of Kronos.

'Are you sure that thing's a good idea?' asked Tim, picking up the gun and handing it gingerly to Hymer as he picked him up off Rob's heavy breakfast. 'We've lost 'im now.'

'Don't worry,' moaned Quakke, putting the gun back into his pocket. 'I know where he's gone.'

Worried was just what Quakke was.

– – –

Despite what seemed an age before they got sorted out and set off in what might be termed 'cold pursuit', Kronos had not got far. As the valiant trio came out of the front of the Antidiluvian Club, causing several heart attacks en route among the elderly members and one or two cases of enuresis, they were relieved to see Sir Julian's chauffeur arguing with a taxi driver who had managed to park his vehicle near enough to the rear of the Daimler to prevent its speedy exodus from the space it occupied. When he witnessed the exit of Quakke and company from the building, he seemed to soften his former intransigence and easing back to let out the Daimler, pulled up in front of the three pursuers. It was not unreasonable to expect miracles, like their dastardly opposites, to come in threes.

Quakke thought quickly.

'Tim, give Rob your car keys. Rob, get off to Henley, please. Find Julie, and make sure she doesn't escape. If Cockney Striker turns up don't confront him – hide or something.'

'Or what?' said Rob. 'Where was it anyway?'

'Henley,' replied Quakke. 'Across the bridge, red, white and blue houseboat, third from the right.'

Quakke bundled Tim into the taxi, believing it was a good idea never to look gift horse power in the mouth.

'Where to, guv?' asked the cabbie, apparently unsurprised at his windfall.

Choked with emotion at finding the moment arrived that most passengers, and cabbies for that matter, can only dream about, Quakke stuttered:

'F...follow that car!'

Whilst, undoubtedly academically challenged and, as we have seen and may do so in the not too distant fure, drastically lacking in judgement, Logos had worked long enough with Kronos to have absorbed most of his methods and to understand his way of thinking. He had donned his disguise as a taxi-driver once more with a view to tailing the three avengers as they left the hotel. With the unmistakeable second clue he had given them, he was expecting to follow them to Henley. Imagine his surprise, therefore, when they had not aimed westwards, but headed for the river. When they finally came to the Antidiluvian Club, it was clear to Logos that Quakke had managed to track down Kronos without using the bait of Julie. It was also clear that Quakke must now have the full picture. Soon it would be time to split. Inside the Antidiluvian Club, he had thought, parking well up the rear of the Daimler while the chauffeur was off for a pot of tea, Quakke was confronting Kronos, and Kronos would have realised that he had, for once, put one over on him.

His heart had missed a beat when he had heard the shot. Kronos would never have used a weapon inside the Club, so... Quakke, or his goons... His hopes were soon dashed as Callendar sped out of the front door and made for his car. What a pity it was hemmed in. From Quakke's hurried instructions which he managed to catch as he reversed to give the Daimler room to manoeuvre, he concluded: he needn't bother about Kaki any more; if Kronos used Quakke to get back Kaki, he would not be too anxious to catch up with Logos himself; and there was no hurry for him to get out of the country. He could still have a bit of fun.

In all three conclusions his judgement was flawed, but was entirely justified by events.

So he had decided to perform one last service to humanity. He had probably confused 'first' and 'last', but to someone whose concern was for himself, first, last, and every ordinal in between, this was of no probable significance. So here he was following the black Daimler, discreetly of course, and listening.

'Where is he going?' asked Tim.

'Banbury, unless I'm much mistaken,' Quakke replied grimly, then to the driver. 'Get a move on, will you? We're nearly losing him.'

'Doin' mi best, guv, doin' mi best,' grumbled the obliging taxi driver.

'To get Lucy, you mean,' clarified Tim.

'Exactly,' Quakke bit his lip.

'I thought you said he was a friend of Lucy's.'

'In principle, yes, but he'd be quite prepared to use her to make us hand over Kaki or at any rate tell him where she is.'

'You think he'd hurt her?'

'To save his own skin, I'm afraid so,' said Quakke, who remembered that Kronos had no principles.

'We should try and get there first, then?'

'Quite so,' replied Quakke. 'Driver, do you know Softwicke Hall by any chance? North of Banbury on the Coventry Road.'

'Went there once with the missus,' said Logos.

'Is there any way you could get there before the Daimler?'

'Do mi best, guv, do mi best,' grumbled the obliging taxi driver.

Logos did indeed know Softwicke Hall and Kronos' "auntie", the stuck-up old bitch and Lucy. He had correctly guessed what the game was. It would tie Quakke and Kronos up for a while and Logos, never to be known by that name again, would escape. There was no way he was going to get to Softwicke Hall first, but to show willing he put his foot down and got nearer to the Daimler. Ten minutes later, to the duo's delight, he overtook it.

Kronos smiled as he saw the taxi with its two occupants go past – for two reasons: Quakke and his companion had guessed his plan; and Quakke, a better General than Kronos, was covering his rear. He had detailed Rob to guard Kaki.

On both counts he was correct in his judgement.

'Just make sure you get there first,' he said to his chauffeur.

Chapter Five

The eleventh Earl Crosse had rebuilt Softwicke Hall in the late eighteenth century largely out of lavish gifts from French aristocrats who had kept their heads from the lantern and its considerably more efficient successor long enough to point them across the Channel. The ennobled gentleman, not particularly warming to the nickname that his activities as a sort of eighteenth century Thomas Cook had earned him, was, nevertheless, proud of his mitigation of what he considered to be the worst of times and did not hesitate to carry on those other activities which in France might then be seen as the prerogative of privilege. Apart from hunting, shooting and fishing, and bedding any likely and unlikely chambermaids, he found time to supervise considerable improvements to the house and grounds. He landscaped the gardens and planted some two hundred varieties of tree, built a new bridge which, even using some of the stones from the old one, cost the princely sum of three hundred pounds, and added two new wings to include new bedroom accommodation and a stuccoed Ballroom.

The reader will note with gratitude that the preceding paragraph was not the prelude to three pages of gratuitous description such as are to be found – research being the last resort of the unimaginative – in some of our modern best-sellers. It was merely a little local colour designed to mark the passage of time between the embarkation of our villain in his Daimler and our heroes (plus another villain) in the taxi and their arrival at the aforementioned late Georgian edifice.

'No sign of him,' said Tim, referring to Kronos.

'No,' said Quakke suspiciously. The taxi was hardly an Indianapolis contender.

'Done mi best, guv, done mi best,' said the cabbie, pulling off the road and onto the mile-long drive which wound its way through woodland to the house high on the hill.

The drive ended in dismay as well as a fine gravelled courtyard.

In front of the large range of steps up to the house was a black Daimler.

'Shall I wait for yer, guv?' asked the taxi driver, obligingly accepting a cheque.

'Thank you, but somehow I don't think that's going to be necessary,' replied Quakke.

Kronos was already waiting for them when the footman opened the huge front door.

'We'll go into the drawing room,' he said. 'You can say "hello" to auntie.

Countess Crosse was always glad to see visitors. She had Quakke before of course.

'And this is Mr... er...'

'Glasby'.

'Not one of the Northamptonshire Glasbys?' enquired the Countess. Tim had to admit his lack of pedigree.

'Well, it's so nice to see you anyway,' said Lady Crosse, 'and Lucy as well. By the way, where is Lucy? I wanted her to take me off for my afternoon nap. Cynthia will have to do it as normal.'

'Lucy was having a little trouble with her car,' said Kronos. 'My chauffeur's seeing to it.'

'Oh well, make yourself at home,' mumbled the old lady.

– – –

She's quite safe,' Kronos assured Quakke, 'just a bit tied up at the moment. Haven't said anything to auntie, of course, don't want her prematurely footing over the pail. I haven't checked what sort of will she's made yet. You could do quite well out of that, Quakke – she adores Lucy. As I was saying, Lucy is quite alright and with a bit of co-operation from you, dear boy, we can have the status quo restored and Lucy back for dinner with the old girl.'

'You bas...'

'Go on, say it!' laughed Kronos, amused by the quaintness of Quakke's inhibitions. 'Actually, it's true. I was brought up in an orphanage in Croydon. Never did find out who my parents were. When I grew up I made sure nobody messed me about again.'

'I'm sorry...' started Quakke.

'Don't be, old boy. Doesn't hurt any more.' He lit a large Havana. 'Sorry, do you...?' The lapse in manners had been only temporary.

Tim shook his head. Quakke took out his pipe and filled it.

He needed the comfort and his grey matter felt devoid of stimulation. He knew what the situation was, but couldn't think of a way out of it. He resorted to display, after the manner of a threatened animal

'If you've harmed one hair of Lucy's head...'

'You'll do what? Get your six-shooter out again? I should throw that in the – what do you call it? – trash-can before you do yourself some damage. Besides, mine's more efficient.'

He took from his pocket a small, but perfectly formed, Browning.

I knew I should have stayed out of this, thought Tim.

I wish I'd stayed out of this, thought Quakke.

'So let's be realistic,' continued Kronos. 'You have something – someone rather that I want. I have someone you want. Shall we do business, gentlemen?'

'What about Freeman?' asked Quakke, playing for time, trying to get his thoughts in gear.

'If we can kill – I use the word in the figurative sense, you understand – if we can kill two birds with one stone, all the better, but I am most anxious for the present to get back my little playmate, as no doubt you are yours. That piece of unmitigated excrement can wait. There's no place on earth he can hide from me after this.'

'Unmitigated exc... what?' whispered Tim to Quakke. He was missing Rob who usually made remarks of this sort.

'I guess he means absolute shit,' Quakke whispered back.

'Right,' said Tim.

'When you've finished your socio-linguistics lesson,' sneered Kronos, 'let's get back to the matter in hand.' So that's what it's all about, thought Tim.

'You don't know the whereabouts of Freeman, I suppose?' enquired Kronos. 'It doesn't matter. As I said, but...' It clearly mattered a great deal.'

'We'd kinda thought he might turn up in Henley,' said Quakke, then wondered whether he should have turned his cards over so quickly.

'Ah, Henley,' said Kronos, 'and the absence of our other young friend...' he was more complimentary now, 'presumably means you are keeping an eye on the young lady. Just in case.'

'Something like that,' grunted Quakke, whose grey matter now told him the futility of trying to hide anything from this man.

'Well then, let's be off,' said Kronos energetically, motioning with the pistol for them to go outside.' We'll take the large Rolls. Lucy's already waiting for us in it, I shouldn't wonder.'

– – –

We need not go into how long it took Rob to get to Henley and find the particular houseboat so graphically, eventually, described by Logos. Looking in his rear-view mirror, or rather Tim's, he kept wondering whether Logos was after him and when he got to the famous boating venue it was the same thing. Look back over the bridge, look back before getting into the half-sinking red, blue and white hulk, look back before opening the rotten, creaking door to the living accommodation where he expected to find some half-dead specimen of humanity – his vocabulary had considerably widened since his association with Quakke.

Even, or especially, perish the thought, bound and gagged, Julie Kerry was beguiling. Rob, like many Yorkshiremen, was naturally racist, believing principally that wogs began somewhere around the outskirts of Sheffield, but this did not extend to lads or lasses with whom he was acquainted and whom he would have died defending whatever the colour of their skin.

The colour of Julie's skin was between olive and what the French describe as café-au-lait, soft, shimmering when exposed to light, silky, velvety – need one say more. She was wearing a little cream suit which brought out the best in her colour and a peach coloured blouse of a thinness through which could be seen the nipples of her breasts. She was lying on a cerise-coloured bench or bunk with her legs and arms tied and there was a tantalising dark patch where her mini-skirt rose nearly to her hips.

Rob coughed as he half-remembered some tale Tim had told him about a dream he had had.

'Are... are tha alreight?' he managed to stammer.

'Uh... uh... uh... uh,' said Julie.

'Ah 'ad a hell of a job findin' thee,' said Rob.

'Uh... uh... uh,' said Julie.

It occurred to him there would be no harm in loosening the gag. He could always pull it up again if anybody, God forbid not Logos, happened to turn up. He did so.

'That's better,' said Julie, breathing deeply. 'You're one of those Yorkshire lads, aren't you?'

''Appen,' said Rob, not wanting to give too much away.

'Have you come to rescue me?'

"Appen,' said Rob, not wanting to give too much away.

'I did a lot of work with the women's support groups, you know.'

'Aye, used 'em more like. Made money aht o' t' job.'

'You see things so black and white,' said Julie, 'things aren't like that down here, you know.'

'Ah've noticed,' said Rob, for reasons we now appreciate.

'That mate of yours,' said Julie, warming to her task. Was Rob imagining things or was she wriggling on the bunk so as to open her legs to the maximum permitted by the bindings.

'Are... are... you comfortable?' asked Rob. 'Yer don't want to go change anything or owt?' He immediately regretted he had said this. He was supposed to keep her prisoner, he thought, not give her a chance to escape. She noticed the consternation.

'No, thank you. Anyway, I don't wear panties or 'anything',' she said, adjusting her position again.

'Fuckin' 'ell,' said Rob to himself for reasons we can appreciate.

'As I was saying,' cooed Julie, 'that mate of yours looks like he could really give a girl a good time.'

'Yer think I couldn't,' said Rob, his manhood hurt. In fact his manhood was beginning to hurt quite badly.

'If you could just take these ropes off my legs...' said Julie.

'Oh, no... er... no... er. Ah've got to go to t' toilet,' spluttered Rob.

He managed to struggle through to what nautical chaps might call the heads, then for a moment lost in imagination... A bang on the door called him to his senses.

'What tha doin' in theer, yer wanker?' asked Tim.

– – –

'Thank God it's thee,' breathed Rob. 'Ah thought it wor that cunt Logos. Ah wor brickin',,'

'Keep thi brown trousers on,' said Tim, 'we've got company.'

Tim led the way back to the lounge where the bunk was now occupied by Quakke and Lucy and the dark beauty was free from all restraint and, pistol in hand, standing next to Kronos who, with HIS weapon, was covering Tim and Rob.

'If we get any more on this boat,' said Rob, 'it'll sink good an' proper.'

'Welcome, gentlemen,' smiled Kronos. 'as you say, it is rather crowded down here, so if you'll forgive us, Julie and I will be on our way. I don't suppose we shall meet again. As three musketeers I am sure you know the difference between "au revoir" and "adieu". I'm so sorry, Lucy. I'm so sorry, Lucy. It's been wonderful all these years, but in the end, on the park, when the fat lady sings, or whatever those dreadful sporting oiks say...'

'It's you or us. You always were a selfish bastard.' Quakke's eyebrows rose visibly. He had never, himself, heard Lucy use bad language.

Kronos smiled. 'How delightfully precise my dear.'

The chauffeur was in turn tying up the four. Lucy's hands had not been untied since she had first been taken off to the garage at Softwicke Hall. Now her feet were tied together as well. The other three – only one of whom was in possession of anything like a musket – covered by both Kronos and Kaki were not in a position to resist. Not strictly true. Rob, who would try anything once, stuck his head rather forcibly into the chauffeur's midriff, but was persuaded by a bullet past his left ear that it might be wise to co-operate. Soon they were all giving a passable impersonation of oven-ready turkeys, which, in view of what was about to happen to them, was not entirely inappropriate.

'That should do nicely,' approved Kronos. 'I am a fair man. You have a very faint chance of survival, very faint – there are not many people around at this time of the year to give any assistance, however hard you shout. Should that faint chance be realised, don't come looking for me again. You're not good at it.'

'Third time lucky,' said Tim, ever the optimist.

'You complete bastard,' said Quakke totally qualmless. The passage about Satan came into his mind.

'That's another fine mess tha's getten me into,' whispered Rob to Tim.

Retreating backwards up the steps after Kaki and the chauffeur, Kronos said 'Adieu!'

There was a loud banging as nails were driven, pinning the cabin door to its jamb.

– – –

Lucy's amazement and incomprehension had been partially cleared up on the journey from Banbury to Henley, but she was still angry with Quakke.

'Why didn't you tell me all this was going on?'

'Just wanted to protect you, sugar. I thought you'd been through enough.'

'It didn't work, did it? I wanted to forget everything, not dredge it all up again. How on earth did you imagine you could do anything against people like these?'

'Well, honey, I thought...'

'You obviously didn't think hard enough,' Lucy chided him, then was glumly silent.

'So near, yet so far,' said Rob dreamily.

'Shut it!' said Tim. 'We've enough on wi' thee tryin' to be a comedian wi'aht philosophy an' all.'

'Guys, guys,' said Quakke, softly.

'If Ah could just get thy hands free wi' my teeth...' said Tim, rolling over on the bunk towards the ropes behind Rob's back.

'They're too bloody thick.'

'See if tha can separate t' strands.'

Several minutes of chewing and spitting produced little result, except a few frayed ends and a bleeding mouth on Tim's part. During this time Professor and Mrs Quakke kissed and made up. They were not going to meet their maker in a state of divorce, however notional, unsure as they still were of the precise form of their demise implied by Kronos.

Tim had rolled back upright. His concentration, released from chewing and spitting, was focussing elsewhere.

'What's that noise?' he said. A cracking was distinctly audible to all four.

'Boat creakin'?' suggested Rob, whose excursions had not included the nautical. 'Hang on...! Oh shit...!' The unmistakeable smell of wood burning brought with it the visible sign of smoke oozing through the badly fitting door and was soon joined by similar manifestations from the galley beyond the cabin.

'Open some winders,' shouted Rob.

'What winders?' said Tim.

'We'll break t' door dahn,' said Rob

'We can't move, yer tuss,' screamed Tim. 'All on yer roll on to t' bloody floor an' yell like buggery.'

Thanks to Quakke's advance in understanding the vernacular, he was able to follow the instructions almost immediately. Lucy got the idea and followed suit.

'Try to keep below t' smoke,' yelled Tim.

The smoke was becoming more intense. There was a feeling of heat. The only relief for the moment was the inch or two of water lying on the planks of the rotting hulk. They were coughing and yelling and yelling and coughing.

Quakke heard the creak and crash of timber and began to pray.

– – –

'Thy will be done, thy will be done...' Quakke was muttering, although his lips seemed to be sticking together and he was conscious of something constricting his face. He tried to pull up his arm to get rid of it, but came up against some restraint, soft and warm, a blanket, and a face was staring down at him and he was moving and there was a stupid siren making a silly noise.

'I should keep that on, sir, if I was you,' advised the man in the green overall, adjusting the oxygen mask. 'Just lie still now, we'll soon 'ave you in a nice warm bed.'

'Lucy...' began Quakke as memory began to return.

'They're all right,' the paramedic assured him, 'or will be at any rate. Somebody must have been on your side. I don't know who got you out of that boat. There was nobody around when we got here. Whoever he was, though, he was a bloody 'ero.'

'Amen,' said Quakke as his head sank back into the pillow.'

– – –

The taxi driver had watched with dismay as the chauffeur, Kaki, and finally Kronos had emerged from the houseboat. Ignoring once again the voice inside himself telling him to get out of the country once and for all, he had felt drawn back to Henley. Hope that the tables might finally be turned on Kronos? Sheer curiosity? The excitement still, after all these years, of covert activity? Who knows. His first instinct, on seeing the chauffeur nail up the cabin door and set fire to the boat before joining the other two in the black Daimler, had been to say to himself, 'Annuver fuckin' cock-up, might as well finish the job meself.' But as he scrambled back to the cab to follow his two erstwhile cronies, something stopped him in his tracks. He looked back at the burning boat and realised that there was only one thing to do and if it wasn't done in a matter of minutes it would be too late.

Fortunately, he was well-attired, mostly in leather of the finest quality, down to the gloves which had long been an indispensable part of his equipment. He suspended his scarf in the water on a boathook, pulled it back up and wrapped it around his face. The door of the cabin, already ablaze, yielded easily to the boathook and he half-dragged, half-pushed the bodies, one by one, out into the air and onto the tow path. Having made sure they were still alive, he left them in the recovery position and called police and ambulance. Only one thing left to do – he quickly drew from his pocket a biro and scrap paper – and then he would be out of the country.

– – –

The effects of the smoke – there were luckily (or providentially?) no burns – soon wore off and, there being a shortage of beds in the Casualty Hospital in York Road, the famous four found themselves discharged. Tim picked up his car and Lucy rang Lady Crosse to say she would not be back for dinner.

'We could go and find a nice little pub. The real ale is very good here, I'm told,' she said temptingly to the two lads.

'Er, I think we have some unfinished business, London-wise,' said Quakke.

'Oh, no. O, oh, no!' protested Lucy. You're not going through all that again.'

'We..ll, you see, honey,' hedged Quakke.

'Why give up when we're winning?' said Rob.

'There's a bit of paper in mi pocket,' said Tim, who not for the first time had found himself used as a letter-box and said so.

'Thi gob's big enough,' taunted Rob.

'It were in mi pocket,' Tim reminded him.

'I'm coming along too,' said Lucy, despite protests from Quakke that she ought to stay out of it. 'At least I can't get kidnapped again.'

– – –

At the Knightsbridge address, scribbled on the piece of paper posted in Tim's pocket, Kaki and Kronos were finishing dinner. The champagne had still not been opened and there was no time for Kronos' favourite substitute. Miss Julie Kerry was shortly to give a talk to the local Women's circle on 'Rape within marriage'.

'We haven't caught up with that rat yet,' said Kronos. 'Looks like we were a bit optimistic about those buffoons getting him for us as well. I ask you, Colt '45!' They both laughed.

'No news from the police, nothing from airports, ports, heliports – nothing. Surely he couldn't get through that security.'

'Well, I don't know,' said Kaki. 'You didn't think he was up to putting somebody on YOUR tail, did you? Perhaps we ought not to underestimate him.'

'That ignorant little shit!' Kronos could still not be convinced that Logos might ultimately come out on top. 'He's still capable of nasty tricks, though. I wish you'd take the car.'

'Nonsense,' Kaki kissed him reassuringly. 'It's only down the road and I need the exercise after being cooped up in that boat.'

'You can have all the exercise you like, when you get back, my angel,' said Kronos, running his hand up her thigh and gently teasing her uncovered groin. 'I don't think we shall have any miner disturbances this evening.'

'Not now,' giggled Kaki, 'I don't want to have to change my dress again. You know how quickly I get wet.'

She kissed him, picked up her handbag and headed for the lift.

– – –

'There's one of the greyhounds out of the trap, anyway,' whispered Tim as he spotted Kaki coming out of the front door and heading towards the

Brompton Road. 'Get out an' follow 'er, Rob, we'll keep a distance behind. We'll follow you, like.'

Rob got out of the car and went along the road, trying to keep a low profile like he'd seen in the films. Unfortunately, he appeared not to have seen enough films. About a hundred yards on, stopping to cross the road, Kaki spotted him. What should she do? The others couldn't be far away. She couldn't use her gun out in the open. A taxi came by and slowed expectantly. She was tempted to get in, then she remembered what had happened last time she had taken a cab. Rob, seeing he had been rumbled, had begun to run. She would have to do likewise. Forgetting in her panic the elementary rules of road safety, she ran round the back of the cab and straight into the path of a Land Rover.

Rob slunk back into the nearest doorway. The driver of the Land Rover and two pedestrians were bending over Kaki.

'I had no chance,' the driver was saying. 'She just came out from behind that taxi. Never saw her till then.'

'She's dead, that's for certain,' pronounced one of the pedestrians. 'We'd better call an ambulance.'

'Did you see that?' asked Rob, as he got back into the car.

'I'm afraid so,' said Quakke, always saddened by tragedy, no matter whom the recipient.

The ambulance came. There were lights and efficient bustlings and noisy sirens. Kronos couldn't fail to notice them. He came out, spoke to the police, then went off and took his own Daimler, following the ambulance.

'Let's get out of here,' said Tim.

– – –

Rob had had nothing to eat since breakfast; neither had the others, but they were not feeling all that hungry. Nevertheless, they were persuaded into a fast food restaurant, where they attempted Mcchicken, Mcfries and Mccoffee, all of which Quakke thought were Mchorrible.

'Ah'll have yours,' offered Rob sifting among the debris on the tiny table.

'We'll give 'im an hour or so to get back 'ome,' suggested Tim.

'OK,' agreed Quakke sadly.

'Why don't we just...?' said Lucy, back in forgiving mode.

'Too late now,' spluttered Rob from the midst of what had once been potato and animal tissue. If we don't get 'im now, we're done for, for certain.'

The others, knowing Kronos as they now did, were forced to admit the cogency of the argument. Anyway, you didn't argue with Rob on a full stomach.

– – –

When they returned to Cardigan Gate, there was no Daimler parked outside.

'We'll give it another 'alf an hour,' decided Tim.

Half an hour later – still no car.

'We'll try the Club,' decided Tim.

They set off for Hyde Park Corner, thence to Piccadilly and Charing Cross. Quakke was already feeling a little sick and he could not ascribe the sensation entirely to the food he had nearly eaten. For comfort he put his hand in his jacket pocket and felt the cold steel. Lucy, next to him in the back of the car, put her arm through his and leant her head on his shoulder.

They managed to pull up outside the Antidiluvian Club without alerting the commissionaire who had popped inside for a warm and locked the door for the moment, it being clear that most of the members who could be expected that evening were already in, including Sir Julian Callendar, who had particularly asked not to be disturbed in the Kitchener Room on the first floor.

'Park right up 'is arse,' advised Rob, who had observed the efficacy of Logos' tactic on their previous visit to the Club. 'Can't see no chauffeur, can you?'

They knew that Kronos had driven himself off to the hospital, but they were wary in case he had been rejoined later by his henchman, particularly since he might be wanting to drown his sorrows. There was no sign of the minion at all, however.

'We'll need rope,' said Tim, getting out and opening the boot of the car.

– – –

When the commissionaire emerged from the front door of the Antidiluvian Club, rubbing his hands and whistling cheerfully after the nice cup of char Mrs Lowndes had given him in the kitchen, he was annoyed to see the Ford Capri parked right up to Sir Julian's Daimler.

''Ere what's goin' on,' he had just time to say to the two young men who emerged from it before Rob headbutted him and Tim tied his arms and legs.

'Where's Callendar?' hissed Tim to the commissionaire before gagging him and bundling him into the back of the Daimler which was not locked. Even criminals knew whose that was and none of them would have dared steal it.

'Kitchener Room, first floor,' gasped the man quickly. Loyalty could not be expected to hold out in all circumstances.

'Carry this other bit of rope,' Tim ordered Rob, as Lucy and Quakke got out of the car. 'Let's get up there before anybody notices there's nobody on the door.'

'Sir!' said Rob, with a mock salute.

There was no-one in the hall. The dining-room was empty. They tip-toed past a couple of elderly generals sleeping off their post-prandial cognacs in the lounge and crept up the stairs. Loud guffaws and tut-tuts from the television room on the left signalled the rest of the occupants of the Club were watching the international football match which Rob had forgotten was on that evening.

'Ah'll just nip an' see what t' score is,' he whispered to Tim.

'Yer daft bat,' said Tim, gentler than usual.

At the end of the corridor was the Kitchener Room.

'I thought I told you no...' started Kronos as he saw the door open, then, 'Well, well it's Wyatt Earp and the posse back from the dead.' Quakke was pointing the six-shooter at Kronos with as steady a hand as he could manage in the circumstances. Kronos, such was his confidence in his own indestructibility, was relaxed enough to joke still.

'Watch the door, Rob,' ordered Tim as he saw Kronos reach for the bell-pull to summon a steward and rushed forward to tackle the Titan. Throwing Kronos into an armchair on the other side of the fire, he dug into his pockets and pulled out the small Browning. He was relieved to see the safety-catch was still on.

'British coal, I hope,' he snarled at Kronos as he withdrew, holding the gun at arm's length and gesturing with his head in the direction of the fire.

'Of course,' mumbled Kronos, winded, but unbowed. He continued, as was his wont, to assume he was in charge of the situation.

Tim had a wary eye on the door. As the handle turned he got behind it and clubbed the astonished chauffeur over the head. Rob tied him up and threw him in a corner.

'One less to worry about,' grunted Tim with satisfaction.

'You ARE improving,' said Kronos, recovering his breath. 'I suppose I must congratulate you on your fortunate escape from the fire. Really against the odds I must say. If I were you, I should fill in a Pools coupon this week. How on earth did you manage it?'

'We had a bit of help,' muttered Quakke, who was not really clear in his own mind what had happened. 'You broke your word,' he continued, feeling some kind of prosecution ought to take place, but still unsure how to proceed.

'Gentleman's agreement, eh?' laughed Kronos. 'Verbal agreement not worth the paper it was written on. You ARE old-fashioned, Quakke. In a sense, however, I have already been punished. Miss Kerry was killed in a road accident this evening.'

'We know,' said Quakke, trying not to sound sympathetic.

'Ah, you know where I live, then?' said Kronos.

'We had a tip-off,' said Tim, showing him the scribbled note.

'Ah,' said Kronos. He would make that rat Logos pay when he finally caught up with him – when he got rid of these nuisances.

'Could I have a drink please?' he asked.

Quakke was still pointing the Colt '45 at him. Tim filled a glass with whisky and handed it to Kronos. Immediately the latter threw the contents of the glass in Tim's face and made a lunge for the bell-pull on the other side of the fire. Tim was spluttering and coughing. He had dropped the pistol. Quakke had a momentary blackout. When he came to, he realised the revolver had been fired and there was an inert heap at his feet.

'I didn't do that, did I?' he mumbled incredulously.

'I told you to be careful with that bloody thing,' said Tim. 'Let's get out of here.'

'Shouldn't I give myself up?' asked Quakke.

'Let's get out of here,' said Tim.

The noise inside the television room had obviously covered all other sounds. They made their way to the first-floor fire-escape and from there to the back of the building. Tim and Rob ran round to get the car. They went back to the hotel in Russell Square and checked out. Soon they were heading for the Midlands.

We need not go into what feelings went through Quakke's mind that night. His make-up is well known to the reader by now. He waited anxiously for the morning paper as Lucy cooked breakfast for the lads who were off back to Yorkshire.

On the front page of the "Morning Bugle" he read:

"TOP CIVIL SERVANT DEAD"

The death has occurred at his Knightsbridge flat of Sir Julian Callendar, Permanent Secretary to the Home Office. It is thought that Sir Julian suffered a massive heart attack. No suspicious circumstances are indicated. His death is particularly tragic, since it came only a few hours after the fatal accident killing his long-time companion, the writer and broadcaster, Ms Julie Kerry. Obituary page 9.

'Bugger me!' exclaimed Rob, assassinating a sausage and looking over Quakke's shoulder.

'No thanks,' said Tim, similarly employed.

'What a waste, though, that Julie. She wor a reight piece o'...' Rob started.

'Aye, a dream,' mused Tim, who knew about such things.

'Don't YOU think it's strange?' Lucy asked Quakke, who seemed determined not to comment.

'Not any more,' replied the Professor who was beginning to understand such things.

– – –

In the dark recesses of the Antidiluvian Club Kronos' epitaph was being formulated.

'Funny business, that,' said Sir Hugh. 'Don't quite understand what went on.'

'Good job we fed the right story to the press, though,' said Lord Slack. 'Couldn't risk blowing the cover of the Special Targets Office.'

'Oh, quite so. Absolutely old thing,' agreed Sir Duckham. 'If these chaps had been arrested, got into a trial or some such tiresome business, where would we have been?'

'Absolutely. Law's an ass. Always said so,' Sir Hugh reminded his companions.

'Useful sort of chap, Julian,' suggested Lord Slack.

'Oh yes, quite,' agreed Sir Hugh. 'Always thought he was a bit too clever for his own good, though, don't you know?'

Nods of approval.

'Chap can do too much thinking,' added Sir Duckham.

Cries of 'Hear! Hear!'.

'Wasn't one of us, really, was he?' continued Sir Hugh. 'Then there was that black woman. Never approved of her. I mean darned fine body an' all that. Used to shag the native girls in Borneo, y'know. Only a bit o' fun though, didn't take 'em seriously.' He paused to wipe his spectacles which were fast steaming up, then continued, 'Once you start taking black women seriously, you're in trouble. Mark my words.'

They did.

'Well, any women, actually,' he finished.

Nods of approval.

'Had some strange habits, by all accounts,' said Sir Duckham thoughtfully. 'Yes, some of 'em very strange.'

Assorted grunts.

'Somebody told me they'd once seen him in a purple suit,' said Sir Hugh, leaning forward confidentially.

The company dissolved into paroxysms of laughter and coughing and more brandy had to be called for to bring them under control.

'It was Freeman who used to wear the purple suit, wasn't it?' asked Slack.

'Was it?' said Sir Hugh, surprised. 'Well, he was a rum cove if ever I saw one.'

'We had some rum coves in the RAF,' volunteered Sir Duckham.

Chapter Six

Winter passed over. The green shoots began to cover all the pleasant land. Even Grimeford lads had now gone back to work and Tim and Rob still had a job – just. What sounds like one of the bad bits of Houseman, and there are plenty, is merely the prelude to the conclusion.

Lucy was fine. She had already started to forget again and Quakke was trying hard not to remember. When the Faminaid envelope came through the letter-box – it must have been during the first week in April – his heart missed at least two beats and was making a rapid ascent into his mouth when he noticed with indescribable relief that the postmark was not Grimeford, but Mbangwa. To his yet more indescribable surprise he saw on opening the missive that it was not asking for a donation, but was a letter from the Director of Faminaid, Franklyn D Freeman. Happy to see a communication from what appeared to be a fellow American, he read on:

'Dear Prof Quake

'Sorry about the monica, the title an' that if you don't recognise me. Ain't got much use for 'em nah. I put all me money into this job an' we got plenty big nobs what can advertise it better van me.

'I done some bad fings in me time, as you know. Funny enough what you was chasin' me for I didn't do on purpose. Gemma's death I mean. I did want to frighten 'er a bit, like. It was the sort of fing we was into ven. We got sort of carried away, then we 'ad to try an' make it look like an accident. But, I expect, being a clever bloke you worked that out by now. I'm glad you got vat bastard vough. He was real evil. I just didn't know what I was doing, really. Well, I fought I did, fought I was on some sort of freedom trip – we all did back in the sixties, fings like vat nasty business wiv vat posh vicar an' vat floppy missus o' yorn. It was really 'im what was in charge, vough. Just like it was when we was got hold of by MI7. I liked the violence, vough, always did, still might do if I let meself, but it was 'im what was in charge. I kept trying to get free, don't yer see? That's why it was my idea to duff Gemma up to be 'onest an' I'm really sorry. What more can I say? Would it have helped if you'd killed me? You didn't seem vat sort, know what I mean? Anyway I'm namin' a 'ospital after 'er if vat's alright wiv you so she didn't die complete for nuffink, vough you probably fink she did still. St Gemma's I'm going to call it.

'As I said, funny fing vis freedom. I fink it started when I dragged you lot out o' the houseboat an' I decided I wouldn't go after that bastard an' 'is tart, 'cos I could make up me own mind, for once, what was importan, know what I mean? Made me fink how many people aren't free. You aren't free over vere as I expect you've realised by now, but you're a 'ell of a lot freer than most of the poor buggers I come across, poor bloody, starving pawns in a power struggle, as I say, like we was, only a million times worse. All power is bad, Mr Quack, that what I had done for me, I tell yer an' as fer vat bastard... Well I digress. I just try an' do me bit now. I don't get involved in no politics, I just pick up the bleedin' pieces, an' I do mean bleedin'. I'm afraid, Mr Quakk.

"Opin vis leaves you as it leaves me an' you can see your way to forgive me for what I done to you an' Mrs Lucy, an' them lads, although I fink the three of you enjoyed the treasure 'unt just a little bit, eh?'

'Your Hobedient servant'

'Fritz'

Quakke blew his nose hard and pondered on the mysterious ways of the world. He decided to stick the letter into his diary with an addendum:

"Man is born free, but is everywhere in chains. It seems that Rousseau's remark is still more than topical. As Freeman says, all types of government are bad – I believe Sir Winston Churchill once said something very similar. Those of us with sophisticated forms must beware of hidden manipulation, we must beware of those who pretend they are acting in our interests, but do not do so. Perhaps, more so, we should fear those who actually believe they know what is best for us. Licence is not freedom and freedom does not mean self-improvement."

From the sitting-room, as Quakke opened the study door, came the strident tones of Jane Green, an economics teacher Lucy had befriended at the local aerobics class.

'Of course, the eighties have brought so many opportunities to women,' she was saying, 'not to mention the consolidation of our sexual freedoms...'

The American closed the door gently and opened another bottle of Jack Daniels.

At the same moment in a muddy ditch in Rwanda, an Englishman lay dying, caught by a mercenary's bullet as he tried to snatch a child out of the way of the victorious Liberation Army.

THE END

Made in the USA
Charleston, SC
01 October 2015